A Dark
Turnover

K.D. McCrite

Annie's®
AnniesFiction.com

Books in the Chocolate Shoppe Mysteries series

Library of Congress-in-Publication Data
A Dark Turnover / by K.D. McCrite
p. cm.
I. Title
2018933872

AnniesFiction.com
(800) 282-6643
Chocolate Shoppe Mysteries™
Series Creator: Shari Lohner
Series Editor: Elizabeth Morrissey
Cover Illustrator: Bonnie Leick

10 11 12 13 14 | Printed in China | 9 8 7 6 5 4 3 2

Prologue

She finally sat down to his favorite dinner and ate a little. The smothered steak was cool by that time, the gravy congealing, the salad limp. She gave up after a few small bites. At least the ice cream in the freezer would still be cold and creamy. Not that she wanted any. Worry, her constant companion, gnawed at her, refusing to be sated.

She glanced at her watch. "Where are you?" she whispered to his empty chair.

The minutes ticked away into hours. She cleared the table and stored the food, then paced from window to window, building scenarios around him until she was exhausted. She sank into a chair, her body weak and trembling, her mind gray and senseless . . .

As the sun cast its first rays through the large picture window, she rose from a fitful sleep and sat up, straining to hear any sounds of his presence in the house. Her gaze out the back window fell on his car parked in the shed and her heart leaped with relief until she remembered he hadn't driven it yesterday.

A quick tour through their small home proved nothing had changed. His bed had not been slept in and his tidy room offered no sign he'd ever been there.

She loved him so much that maybe she had loved him too much.

He had told her to let him have his space and his freedom or he'd leave. But she had pestered and hovered constantly. Boys coming home from the war had problems, and he was no different. She was worried about him.

She caught her refection in the mirror above his dresser. The pale, drawn face staring back was unfamiliar, the eyes filled with the knowledge of his promise now fulfilled.

Look what I've done. He may never come home again.

And he didn't.

Jillian Green had just made fresh coffee when her best friend, Savannah Cantrell, entered The Chocolate Shoppe Bakery quietly, head down, blotting her nose with a tissue.

"Don't tell me you're having some kind of wedding-planning crisis," Jillian said as she tucked a stray lock of curly red hair behind her ear. "I know James isn't getting cold feet. Is he?"

Savannah met her gaze, tears in her eyes and clinging to her lashes. Even tearful, the mahogany-haired, brown-eyed Savannah was beautiful. Silently, she shook her head. Of course James Wilson wouldn't have second thoughts about marrying her. He was a settled and respectable member of the community now, not the fickle boyfriend Jillian had been crazy about in high school. He loved Savannah and proved his devotion every time they were together.

Jillian felt foolish for even asking such a thing. She clunked down the coffeepot and hurried to her friend. "What's wrong? Sit down."

Savannah wiped her eyes and sat at one of the small tables. "I just found out . . ." She swallowed hard, then sniffed and cleared her throat. "I just found out that Rita Carter has c-cancer."

Jillian sat down hard. "Not Miss Rita."

"She just told me." Savannah's voice cracked.

"But . . ." Jillian fought for words and found them lacking. "She's always been so healthy, so strong."

"I know. She has always called herself a 'tough ol' gal.'"

"Surely she can fight this. Do you know her prognosis?"

Savannah's tears spilled down her cheeks. "Not good. She can't fight it. She's got a few weeks left at best."

"No!"

At the sound of Jillian's loud protest, Bertie Harper—her feisty, blonde-haired grandmother and the owner of The Chocolate Shoppe Bakery—glanced over from the cash register, where she'd just sold a dozen doughnuts.

She hastened across the room when she saw their faces. "What's wrong? Both of y'all look like bad news twice over. What's happened?"

"It's Miss Rita," Jillian said.

Savannah nodded and blew her nose. "Terminally ill."

Bertie sat down in the nearest chair, her gaze never leaving Savannah's face. Lenora Ryan, the resident master baker, stepped out of the kitchen and saw them. She lost her smile, and her broad face became serious.

"Girls? What's happened?"

Savannah drew in a deep breath, blurted the news, then broke into sobs.

"Oh, dear. Oh, goodness." Lenora shook her head.

"She's been around for a long time." Maudie Honeycutt spoke up from her place a couple tables away. She and her best friend, Wanda Jean Maplewood, never hid their appetite for eavesdropping and gathering news or rumors. She plucked absently at a strand of her snow-white hair. "How old is she now?"

"Ninety-one last January." Savannah spoke around her weeping.

"She's had a good, long life." Wanda Jean sighed.

Lenora blinked hard. "One of the pillars of this community."

"She was my favorite teacher," Jillian said.

"She's everyone's favorite teacher," Savannah said. "Fifty years is a long time to be doing one thing."

"It surely is." Bertie had been in the baking business about that long. "You don't do something for that many years unless you're good at it, and you love it."

"Or you learn to love it," Lenora added. "Gotta stick to it for a while to become good at it, no matter what."

"I've been pretty close to Miss Rita these last few years," Savannah said, "especially since she asked me to do bookkeeping for her."

"Bookkeeping?" Wanda Jean said. "What kind of bookkeeping?"

Bertie frowned at the woman. "I'm sure Savannah does not want to share that information."

"It's confidential." Savannah sniffled again.

"Oh." Wanda Jean blinked as if she'd never considered any information to be confidential. She tipped her head to one side, and the sunlight caught the silver strands in her thick salt-and-pepper bun. "I reckon she's been keeping secrets all these years. Of course, her being alone for so long and not having anyone to spend money on—"

"Now, Wanda Jean, you hush. This isn't the time for speculation." Bertie pinned a flinty gaze on her, and the woman snapped her mouth shut.

"Is she in the hospital?" Maudie asked.

Savannah shook her head and dabbed her eyes. "There's nothing they can do for her, and as long as she can be at home, she wants to stay there."

"But she hasn't got any family. You can't call Boone Hackett family." Wanda Jean leaned toward them. "I know for a fact that—"

"I plan to drop by every day," Savannah said before Wanda Jean could continue with whatever fact she thought she knew. "I'll stay with her, if it comes to that. I won't let Miss Rita die in that house all by herself."

"You're a good girl, honey." Bertie smiled and patted Savannah's hand. "I'll make sure she isn't lacking for anything, meal-wise."

"That's right." Lenora nodded vigorously. "We'll keep her fed."

Maudie raised a hand. "I'll be happy to pitch in and help with the meals."

"Thank you, Maudie," Bertie said. "That would be a blessing."

"I'll take her some magazines," Wanda Jean offered. "I have two years' worth of *Tattletale Times* she can have."

Lenora scowled. "Miss Rita won't be interested in any of those silly old tabloids."

"You don't know that. There's some interesting stories in those magazines. That's why I've kept them."

"Don't take her any dusty old gossip rags," Bertie said. "You'll make her sicker than ever."

"I get woozy just reading the headlines when I'm checking out at the grocery store," Lenora said. She had a humorously direct way about her that soothed an aching heart.

"Me too." Jillian glanced at Wanda Jean, who seemed a little wounded. "I bet she'd like magazines that have birds and flowers and pretty houses."

"She would," Savannah agreed. "And poetry books. She loves poetry."

"All right. I'll see what I can find." There was determination in Wanda Jean's tone.

Lenora lifted her head and sniffed. "I better check those turtle brownies. Don't want to overbake them."

"You have a good sniffer," Bertie said. "I can always trust you not to let anything scorch."

The bell above the front door tinkled and four giggling preteen girls came in.

"Uh-oh," Jillian said. "That little quartet can create some problems if we aren't careful. A couple of days ago, they emptied all the sugar packets into a cup and poured creamer on top of it for no reason at all."

"They're feeling their oats," Bertie said. "Thank goodness,

school will be starting up soon and they'll have more productive things to do. I'll keep my eye on them. You stay here with Savannah." Bertie touched Savannah's shoulder lightly, then stood up. "Good morning, ladies," she said cheerfully to the girls, who giggled even louder. "I have a nice table for you right here in front. Now, you sit there and I'll bring you your order, like in a café. What can I get for you?"

Savannah wiped her eyes. "Miss Rita delivered this news to me over the phone. I wanted to go over there immediately, but she said no. She said she has some things to do first."

"She has spent so much time alone as she's grown older," Jillian said, "so maybe she wants to process this in her mind, alone."

Savannah plucked at the tissue, making a soft mound of white, papery bits. "She wants me to drop by after church on Sunday, before the Sweetie Pies meeting. I asked if I could bring you along, and she said please do. So will you go with me?" She peered at Jillian, her eyes pleading as if she thought Jillian might refuse.

"Of course I'll go with you. I love Miss Rita, and I need to visit with her now, before . . . well, you know."

Savannah nodded. "Thank you."

"I feel bad about not going to see Miss Rita before now," Savannah said as she drove them across town after church the following Sunday. "It's been almost a week since she told me about her diagnosis."

Jillian leaned down to adjust the thin strap on her red Mary Jane high heels. What had she been thinking when she bought the wretched things? They were too snug, too high, too red, and too expensive. But they did look nice with her sleeveless cream-colored dress and, with the thin red belt she wore, they made her feel as though she'd stepped out of the 1940s. And they had been marked down forty percent. How was she expected to resist a deal like that?

"Kindly remind yourself that she told you not to come until today." Jillian straightened. "Whatever you do, Savannah, don't feel guilty on any level about this situation. It's a normal reaction that friends have, but all it will do is make the time we have left with her dismal. We need to enjoy these days with her."

"It's going to be hard to stay pleasant and cheery. I doubt I can pull it off one hundred percent of the time."

"No one could do that. It's tough to face the future. It's hard enough to deal with the present sometimes."

Savannah swallowed hard. "Well, I'll do my best to comfort her in her mind and spirit, even if no one can stop what's happening to her body."

"So will I. So will Bertie and Aunt Cornelia, and all the others who care about her." Jillian glanced in the back seat. "I hope she enjoys those cherry turnovers. They are her favorite goodie from the bakery, especially when they have lots of glaze on top."

Savannah nodded. "She's not having any measures to prolong her life, though I wish she would. Maybe she'll still enjoy her food. It was wonderful of Bertie and Lenora to bake them special."

"Isn't that just like those two?" Jillian smiled. "Savannah, you know what?"

"I know a lot of things, but to what are you referring specifically?"

"We are blessed to have such wonderfully strong, vibrant, and courageous women in our lives."

"Yes, we are." Savannah pulled into the gravel driveway of Miss Rita's small gray house.

The lawn had recently been mowed, and impatiens bloomed

in the flower boxes beneath the windows. Red geraniums hung in pots along the edge of the porch. The chains on the porch swing creaked quietly, moving it back and forth in the warm afternoon breeze. To look at the place, no one would ever know the energetic Rita Carter would soon be gone.

Savannah gazed through the windshield at the house. "Now it's our turn to be wonderfully strong, vibrant, and courageous."

Miss Rita Carter was a tiny woman who, in her best days, had stood at a towering five feet and one inch, and weighed, at her heaviest, one hundred pounds. The years had shrunken her body but not her mind or spirit. Dressed in a navy-blue dress with a pleated skirt and with her hair swept back in a neat chignon, she appeared as healthy and vigorous as ever. Jillian had hardly anticipated the woman being weak, but she hadn't expected her usual moxie either.

"Good afternoon, girls," Miss Rita sang out. "Come on in."

Savannah kissed the woman's cheek, and Jillian gave her a warm hug.

"It's so good to see you again, ma'am," Jillian said.

"You too, dear. You're looking well." She ran her gaze along Jillian and halted at the shoes. "Gracious, those shoes! I wish I could wear red heels again. But years of being on my feet, teaching and so forth—" She shook her head and indicated an off-white chenille sofa. "Have a seat, won't you? Would you prefer coffee or sweet tea? I have both."

"Sweet tea, please, Miss Rita," Savannah said.

Jillian seconded the request, then held out the box of turnovers. "Bertie and Lenora sent you a gift."

Miss Rita peered through the cellophane window on top of the bakery box and smiled. "My favorite. Bless their hearts. Please thank them for me. I'll go get your tea."

"Let me do that, Miss Rita." Savannah made a move for the kitchen.

The elderly woman's sharp blue eyes met hers. "I can do it, and I will do it as long as I am able. But thank you."

Savannah sat down on the sofa as Miss Rita left the room. She bit her lower lip.

"You have to let her do it her way, Savannah," Jillian whispered.

"I know. But I want to help as much as I can."

"Then help by allowing her to feel and act like herself for as long as she can. If I know Miss Rita, she'll tell you when she needs you."

"You're right." Savannah let out a long sigh.

Jillian glanced around and took in the small, neat room with its off-white sofa and chintz chairs. "It hasn't changed much over the years, has it?"

"Not much."

Porcelain birds sat on crisp white doilies that protected the wooden end tables. A bouquet of silk summer flowers in shades of yellow sat in the center of a small, oval coffee table. Across the room were shelves of books and several framed photographs. On the center shelf sat an eight-by-ten framed photo of a young man in an Army uniform. On either side of him was a white candle.

In Jillian's memory, nothing else had ever been on that shelf. "Her son was a handsome young man, wasn't he?" she said to Savannah.

"He was. Miss Rita showed me a picture of her husband one time. Ryan looked a lot like him."

"I don't think I've ever seen a picture of Mr. Carter."

Savannah lowered her voice. "And you're not likely to. He left when—"

"Here we are." Miss Rita rolled in a small tea cart with their beverages on ice and the turnovers on a plate.

"That is the quietest tea cart I've ever seen," Jillian said with a smile. "Ours sounds like something that's been run up and down the road, hauling hay."

They all laughed as Miss Rita passed out the refreshments.

"This one might squeak too, but Boone keeps everything around here in good working order, God bless him," she said. "That boy has been a godsend."

"He surely has," Savannah agreed.

Boone Hackett could hardly be called a boy, though. Sixty-five if he was a day and still single, he had grown up and still lived in a house just a few doors down from Miss Rita. He had been lifelong friends with her son, Ryan. For as long as Jillian could remember, Boone worked in the produce department of Food for Less. He attended Moss Hollow Fellowship Church from time to time, but never really participated in anything except the semiannual workday, when the grounds were spruced up and any needed repairs were made to the building. Quiet and well-mannered, he had always blended into the background.

"Jillian, do you still like to read?" Miss Rita asked.

"Yes ma'am, I do."

"I remember you borrowing my *Little House on the Prairie* books, and often."

"I read them so many times I think I memorized parts of them. And I love the Garth Williams illustrations. He made the stories come even more alive."

Miss Rita smiled and nodded. They enjoyed the tea and turnovers, and chatted about Miss Rita's lovely flower bed and window boxes until she set her glass aside and met Jillian's eyes. "I'm sure Savannah has told you my news."

"Yes ma'am, she has." Jillian swallowed hard and forced herself to match Miss Rita's composed demeanor. "I am so sorry."

The woman waved one small, fine-boned hand. "Don't be. This ending of life is simply a part of it, and I have had many years more than most." She offered a smile. "I'm ready to go when my Maker calls me. I've been prepared for a long time." She patted her heart, then tapped her temple. "But I realize there is more to the end of one's life on the earthly plane than simple death."

Simple death? Jillian blinked at the phrase. She wasn't sure she was prepared to think of life's end in those terms. Dating a mortician had helped her view it differently, but she still couldn't see it as simple, especially for those it left behind.

Miss Rita continued, "I've called Savannah here for more than a glass of cold tea on a warm day."

"Yes ma'am," both younger women responded, as if they were still in her classroom.

The older woman gave Savannah a warm smile. "My dear, you have helped me so much these last few years. Especially with the paperwork that had to be handled."

"I was happy to do it for you, Miss Rita. You know that."

"Yes, I know. But I'm not happy about it."

Savannah's eyes widened. "Oh? Did I make an error? If you'll give me everything, I'll see if I can—"

"Hush, child, and let me speak."

"Yes ma'am." Savannah sat back.

"You have spent hours working on this for me because you know my eyes are weak."

"Yes ma'am, but I—"

Miss Rita raised her hand again. "No talking."

Savannah clamped her lips into a thin line.

"You flat refused to let me pay you for your work and for your time."

"Oh, but—"

"I realize you did me a great service, and you did it out of respect for me."

"Yes ma'am, because I really do love you," Savannah said as fast she could before the retired teacher hushed her again.

Miss Rita bowed her head for a moment, and when she lifted it, unshed tears glistened in her eyes. "I want to give you something. And as a well-bred Southern girl, you know you cannot decline a gift from a dying woman."

Savannah frowned. "Now, Miss Rita, what are you up to? You shouldn't—"

"Jillian, you are in charge of keeping your friend quiet until I've said my piece and made my peace."

"Yes ma'am." What else could Jillian say? Miss Rita was a force to be reckoned with, even at ninety-one years old and dying from a terminal illness.

Miss Rita reached into the pocket of her blue skirt and pulled out a leather fob with two keys. She traced them with a fingertip, then held them out to Savannah. When Savannah merely stared at her, the woman shook the fob, making the keys jingle.

"Take it," Jillian murmured.

Savannah silently reached out and accepted the offering. The letters *RC* had been tooled into the leather.

Miss Rita cleared her throat and blinked rapidly. "So many of the boys in Vietnam were welcomed home with coldness or resentment, even outright hostility, when all they had done was obey orders handed down from the leaders of the country. They deserved better."

"Yes ma'am, they did," Jillian said quietly.

"I refused to let my Ryan return and think his mother felt the war had changed him into some kind of villain. Growing up was hard enough on him." She stared at nothing while her mind traveled for a while. Then she blinked and focused once more on Savannah. "I bought that for him." She dipped her head toward the keys, her gaze on them. "I wanted to get just the right welcome-home present, so I took Boone with me and we went car shopping. He showed me what he said was Ryan's dream car. Oh my, it was beautiful." She leaned forward, a smile on her lips. "Just between us, I think it was as much Boone's dream car as it was Ryan's. 'It has Ryan's name written all over it,' he said. 'From the paint color to the upholstery to that AM/FM radio.' We took it out for a test drive, Boone and I, and then I bought it for my boy, brand spanking new, right off the showroom floor." She transitioned slowly from bittersweet memories into the present. "I want you to have that Buick, Savannah. It's yonder, out in the old shed."

Savannah blinked at her. "Miss Rita!"

The elderly woman peered at her over the top of her glasses, then got to her feet. "Come with me, and I'll show you."

A car in the old shed? Jillian and Savannah exchanged a glance.

"Come along!"

The crisp voice shook them out of their astonishment. They got to their feet and followed her.

The shed sat farther back in the lot, at the end of the driveway. It was square, with peeling white paint and windows that had long ago been boarded shut. Even with the lawn neatly trimmed and the black-eyed Susans and hollyhocks blooming around its foundation, the old building had always seemed out of place.

"Ryan parked that car in there the last day he was home," Miss Rita said as they walked. "There were no doors on the shed in those days. When a few months went by without a word from him, people started asking me if I'd like to sell it. Calling me at all hours, mind you. And dropping by. Of course I wasn't going to sell his car. He'd need it when he got home. One morning, I got up and spotted two men in the shed when I went out to the mailbox. They had the hood up and were poking around in the engine. A third man was in the driver's seat, running his grubby fingers all over the nice upholstery."

"You mean they just came right onto your property without asking?" Savannah asked.

"That's what I mean. Trespassing. Telling me they would 'take it off my hands.' Going on and on about how Ryan had probably gone for good so I didn't need two cars. You better believe I ran them off in no uncertain terms. I told them if they set foot on my place again, I'd call the sheriff."

"Good for you," Jillian said.

Miss Rita pointed toward the shed. "So I had Boone build those double doors, then put on that heavy lock and chain. And I had him nail boards over the windows for good measure. That kept the snoops out, but it took awhile before they quit calling or coming by. I thought about getting a dog. You know, one of those big ones that bark at people. But I didn't want to discourage my friends from visiting."

The women came to a stop in front of the large double doors held shut with a thick chain and padlock, now crusted with rust. The old shed had been closed up, but it had a dirt floor, and the doors didn't rest snugly against the ground.

Miss Rita stared at the chain. "I haven't been inside the shed since the day I locked these doors."

Nearly half a century had passed, and the building had not been opened in all that time? Once again, Jillian and Savannah exchanged glances. What else would be inside? Spiders? Wasps? A snake or two? An uneasy shiver skittered down Jillian's backbone.

Miss Rita fished in her skirt pocket once more and pulled out a single key attached to a faded blue ribbon. She struggled to insert it into the lock, although Jillian was unsure if the trouble came from the rust or from her trembling fingers.

"Here, let me help with that." Jillian took the key and, with some effort, was able to open the padlock. She handed the key back to her former teacher.

Miss Rita returned the key to her pocket. "Thank you, dear. Now, if we can just open these old doors, we'll see what's inside."

Jillian tugged on one door, and Savannah helped Miss Rita

with the other. The hinges scraped and creaked like fingernails on a chalkboard, then relented slowly with the women's efforts. Opening the doors unleashed the musty odor of old things stored, revealing a space full of tools, boxes, mud-daubers nests, spiderwebs, and plenty of dust and dirt.

Sunlight streamed through thin gaps between the wooden boards, causing narrow light stripes to rest on dust-covered bottles, cans, and old machine parts. But what really captured their attention was the army-green tarp that formed a large mound in the center of the building.

"Pull off that cover, girls," Miss Rita said.

Jillian glanced down at her pale dress. This was only the second time she'd worn it, and the decades of dirt she was bound to get on it would probably never come out. Plus, she doubted there'd be time to change before the Sweetie Pies meeting that afternoon. In fact, she figured both she and Savannah would need hot showers, if not complete decontamination.

"Don't be a princess," Savannah murmured. "Grab that end, and I'll get this side."

She ran her gaze over Savannah's linen slacks and blue top, then relented. After all, she wanted to help Miss Rita. Clothes could always be laundered or dry-cleaned.

Swatting aside spiderwebs as they went, they moved to the far end of the shed, one on each side of the car, and took hold of the corners of the filthy tarp. Walking backward like models displaying prizes on a game show, they pulled the cover off the car, revealing first the back bumper and trunk. Then they let it slide off the rest of the way, exposing the hood and headlights.

Jillian's eyes went large. "Oh. My. Goodness."

Savannah said nothing at all, but when Jillian glanced at her, she was equally wide-eyed. Miss Rita stood to one side, palms pressed together, fingertips to her lips as though praying.

All three women stood, unmoving, staring at something that might as well have been transported through a time machine. Protected from decades of dirt and dust, and as red as the sweet cherry filling in Lenora's and Bertie's turnovers, the paint shone like a polished mirror.

"It's a 1972 Buick Riviera," Miss Rita said.

"Yes ma'am." After a short, nearly reverent silence, Savannah said, "Miss Rita, are you *sure* you—"

The elderly woman peered over the top of her glasses to meet Savannah's gaze. It was a gesture she'd used often in school, and it always brought silence and order to the classroom. "I'm sure it's a collector's item. If you don't want to keep it, then feel free to sell it."

Savannah reached out one tentative hand and touched the curve of the fender. "Oh, no. Never. I love it."

Miss Rita's stern expression relaxed into a smile. "Good. But if you ever find yourself in need of money, I believe this will bring it in quickly." Her smile faded and the corners of her mouth drooped. "I've given up on Ryan ever coming home. And by now, even if he did, I doubt he'd want it. I'm sure he moved on to the bigger and better things he always wanted, which I could never provide. I thought the car might make up for . . . well, never mind."

Jillian had only a passing knowledge of Miss Rita's son, who had disappeared before she was born. Even Maudie and Wanda Jean never spoke of Ryan Carter. "What happened back then, Miss Rita?" The words slipped out of her mouth before she realized she'd even thought them.

Savannah gaped at her. "Jillian!"

Miss Rita held up one hand to hush her. "No, no, Savannah. I'm glad she asked. It shows she cares."

"Yes ma'am, I do care," Jillian said. "And if you'd rather not talk about it, I understand. I don't mean to pry."

"Don't give it a second thought." The woman glanced at

her wristwatch. "Gracious! The Sweetie Pies meeting starts in a few minutes, and you don't want to be late. But you come back sometime, and I'll tell you about Ryan. Come on out of this old shed." She led the way outside and waited while they closed the doors and secured the padlock.

"Would you like to go along with us, Miss Rita?" Savannah asked. "I know it's been years since you came to a meeting, but it'd be fun."

"Not today. I have some things to catch up on." She glanced toward the house, a slight frown marring her expression.

"Would you like us to stay and help you?" Jillian asked.

"Absolutely not. Bertie and Cornelia would never forgive me for keeping you away from a Sweetie Pies meeting." She laughed and made a shooing gesture. "Now, go on. Scoot."

Still, they hesitated.

"Miss Rita." Savannah took in a deep breath, then gathered the woman in a full but gentle embrace. "Thank you for the gift. I don't know what to say other than that you're wonderful, and you always have been." She blinked back tears as she straightened.

Miss Rita smiled at her tenderly and patted her cheek as if Savannah were still in fourth grade. "No, I'm not, and no, I haven't always been. If I'd always been wonderful, Ryan would not have left." She stepped back. "Now, you go. Jillian, make her leave. I have things to take care of."

Miss Rita's words and the look in her eyes disturbed Jillian. "Will you call us when you need us?" she asked.

"I will." Miss Rita shooed them toward the car.

"I don't like this," Jillian said when they got in Savannah's sedan. "Going off and leaving her alone."

"Neither do I."

"I wish I hadn't asked about Ryan. She was all right until then."

"I know."

"Maybe we should stay, whether she wants us to or not."

Savannah shook her head and started the car. "I've been around Miss Rita enough to know that if we force our company on her when she so obviously wants us to go, we'll upset her even more."

Jillian gazed out at the tidy house. "Then we should come back after the meeting."

"Okay. But I'll call first and see how she is. She may not want us around then any more than she does right now."

Leaving the older woman alone certainly seemed less than ideal, but Savannah was far more familiar with Miss Rita's habits and ways of doing things than Jillian was. All Jillian could do was wait. And worry.

The moment the Southern Sweetie Pies meeting adjourned, Wanda Jean turned to Savannah and Jillian. "Both of you were late getting here today. What did you find out over at Rita's? Is she feeling any better?" She popped one of Annalise Reed's bite-size pecan tartlets into her mouth and chewed as she watched them with an expectant glimmer in her eyes.

Jillian's great-aunt Cornelia gave the woman a quizzical stare. "Why, I don't believe there is any 'feeling better' when a person has a terminal illness."

Wanda Jean dusted crumbs from her fingers. "Yes, you're right about that. I should have asked how she's feeling today."

"She seems in remarkably good spirits," Savannah said.

"Far better than I would be if I were in her shoes," Jillian added.

"I wish she was still attending the meetings," Bertie said. "I've missed her since she stopped coming to the Sweetie Pies. But I know she has her reasons."

"I wish she hadn't stopped coming before I moved back to Moss Hollow," Jillian said. "Anyway, she appeared to be plenty energetic. She said she had things to do. And she was all dressed up, so I think she must have attended church this morning."

"Does she still go to Rock Valley Methodist?" Annalise asked.

"She's gone there all her life, just like Stewie Franks," Maudie said. "She'll be faithful to Rock Valley until the end, even though it's two miles out in the country and down that little dirt lane."

"She doesn't drive anymore, but Stewie, Pastor Julie, or her husband always picks up Miss Rita every Sunday and takes her there," Cornelia said. Although she was Bertie's twin sister, the resemblance stopped at their physical appearance. Cornelia was flighty and whimsical, while Bertie was sensible and pragmatic.

"I do believe she'd walk if someone didn't take her," Maudie added.

"She's deeply rooted in that church," Bertie said. "Her father pastored at Rock Valley for thirty years or longer. And she had a fair say when Pastor Julie was hired."

"Miss Rita is a remarkably strong, brave person," said Laura Lee Zane. She was currently a deputy with the Moss Hollow sheriff's department, and she baked the best crescent rolls Jillian had ever tasted. "A few years ago, when someone tried to break into her house through the kitchen window, she called the sheriff's office and asked for one of us to come and pick him up. She said we might need to bring smelling salts or maybe a stretcher, because she'd laid him out with her three-gallon soup kettle."

This brought a burst of laughter.

"That sounds like our Miss Rita," Savannah said.

"I remember the time she took us on a hike out to Red Rim Cave to study bats when we were in her class," Jillian said. "Nearly wore all us kids down to nubs, but she never even got out of breath. Remember that, Savannah?"

"Do I ever. She was still taking kids on field trips to that cave right up until she retired."

"Did you see any bats?" Wanda Jean asked.

"We saw more bats in that cave than I ever want to see again," Savannah said with a shudder.

"God bless her," Bertie said when the laughter subsided. "Rita Carter will be missed."

"Yes she will." Maudie tilted her head to one side and eyed Jillian. "So, did she have any special reason for inviting you two over there today?"

"She served us sweet tea." Jillian smiled at Lenora and Bertie. "She was thrilled with your turnovers."

"I know she has always loved them," Lenora said. "I'll make sure she has plenty from here on out."

Savannah glanced at her watch. "I'm going to give her a call, see how she's doing." She excused herself and stepped away from the group. When she returned a short time later, she said, "She says she's feeling all right but tired, and doesn't want callers this evening. She hopes everyone understands."

"Of course we do," Bertie said, and the others agreed.

"But I'll keep my eye on her," Savannah promised again. "Every day."

"Ever since I can remember, she's liked her quiet time," Cornelia said. "Maybe she has a visitor from the Other Side, like I do."

Here we go again. Cornelia had decided her late husband, Raymond, somehow spoke to her through Bertie's cat, Possum, giving guidance and ominous warnings of things to come. The Sweetie Pies knew this and did their best not to foster the woman's fanciful meanderings. Right then, no one encouraged her to tell them more about her visitor from the "Other Side," and she let the subject drop.

The women continued to reminisce about Miss Rita, remembering her days as a teacher who had reached at least three generations of students. The words were a tribute to a good woman. Bittersweet warmth settled over them while the memories flowed.

The talk dwindled, and Savannah met Jillian's eyes. "Should I tell them about the car?" she mouthed.

"Sure," Jillian said quietly. "Tell them."

"Tell us what?" Wanda Jean asked immediately, as if Jillian had shouted.

Savannah cleared her throat. "Miss Rita gave me something today while we were there."

This announcement halted all movement, piqued curiosity, and drew interested gazes to her.

"What did she give you?" Maudie prodded. "A keepsake? She has some lovely old things in that house."

"Yes, she does, and yes, I guess you could call her gift a keepsake."

"Well, good gravy, stop beating around the bush and tell us." Wanda Jean practically writhed in anticipation.

Savannah pulled the keys to the Riviera out of her purse and dangled them from the fob. "This is what she gave me."

The women gaped at the keys.

"That seems like a peculiar gift," Cornelia said. "Why would she give you keys?"

"You do beat all," Bertie said, frowning at her sister. "Sometimes I don't believe you think before you speak."

"Piffle." Cornelia waved dismissively.

"Those are car keys," Laura Lee said.

Lenora frowned. "She gave you her car? Why, honey, I thought she sold it when she stopped driving a few years ago."

"Not that car. These are the keys to a beautiful red Buick Riviera that has been in her shed since the early '70s."

"Isn't that the one she bought for Ryan when he got back from Vietnam?" Bertie asked.

"It is." Maudie nodded vigorously. "And it cost a pretty penny, let me tell you. I remember seeing him and Boone in that car several times after he got out of the service. They'd circle the square downtown, then go up and down every street in Moss Hollow, making sure everyone saw them. What a sight that was—windows down, Boone with his long black hair blowing around his head. Ryan grew his hair out quick enough after he was out of the service too."

"All the boys had long hair back then," Bertie said.

"And big old muttonchops. Remember them?" Lenora asked, and the women tittered about long hair and whiskers for a minute.

"Clarence had them, and an afro that was bigger than a basketball." She faced Savannah. "So Miss Rita still has that car?"

"She does. She held onto it for so long because she hoped Ryan would come back."

"Bless her heart," Cornelia murmured.

Wanda Jean had been silent for a while, but her curious stare was fixed on Savannah. "You mean to say she just up and gave you that car?"

Savannah glanced at the keys. "She did."

"I declare." Wanda Jean gazed around at the others with wonderment on her face. "I thought she'd gotten rid of that thing a long time ago. I would have sold it. Imagine keeping it a secret all this time."

"She was hardly keeping it a secret," Jillian said. "She's been hoping her son would come back."

"Oh, him." Maudie shook her head. "She's been better off without him, if you want to know the honest truth."

"I don't know if I'd go that far," Bertie said. "After all, he's her son and she loves him very much. But I do know that boy was always trouble for her. When his draft number came up and he went off to the Army, everyone thought it might settle him down—"

"If he came back alive, you mean," Cornelia added.

"—and it did settle him, for a while," Bertie said, with a glare at Cornelia. "Then one of the boys he was in the service with showed up a couple of months later, and Ryan took to his old ways, unpredictable as all get-out and running around." Bertie shook her head slowly. "When the two of them took off for parts unknown without a word to anyone, poor Miss Rita went on with life as best she could, always expecting him to come home any day."

"But Boone's still here," Jillian said. "Weren't they good friends? Didn't he know where Ryan went?"

"I suppose not, or he would've told her."

"Ryan just up and left her, same as that rotten Marvin Carter did while Ryan was still a baby," Maudie said. "Walked out and never came back. Like father, like son."

"I never knew that," Jillian said. "Did you, Savannah?"

Savannah jumped up from her chair and walked to the nearly empty coffeepot as though she meant to fill her cup. "That's terrible!" she cried. "Miss Rita did not deserve that much pain in her life." With her hands curled into fists and visibly fighting tears, she whirled to face the others. "The rest of us should make sure her last days are her best days."

"Well, honey," Bertie said softly, "that's what we plan to do."

That evening, Jillian sat on her bed with her laptop. She pulled up an Internet search engine and typed in *Ryan Carter*. The name had a lot of hits, and she kept trying to narrow her search by age, location, and service record. All she found was a birthdate of a Ryan Carter in Nathan County, Georgia, but nothing else.

She called Savannah and told her what little she had found. "Do you know his middle name? Maybe that would help, though I doubt it."

"I don't know it," Savannah said. "James and I have tried for hours to find information about him online, but we ran into the same problem. James thinks he probably changed his name, and I'm inclined to agree with him."

Jillian groaned. "I had the same thought. Well, what about that friend of his that was in the service with him? What was his name?"

"Miss Rita has never told me his name, and I haven't asked.

There are some things that just seem too painful for her, and I think that guy is one of them."

"Maybe. At any rate, I'm not ready to give up just yet. I'll keep digging. She really needs to see her son before she dies." Jillian winced as she expressed her next thought. "Savannah, have you considered that he might be dead?"

"I hate to say it, but yes. I've considered that possibility."

"Given the kind of people he was running around with, do you think it could be that he fell into bad company?"

"I'd say that's likely. Think about it. If he were still alive, he surely would've reached out to Miss Rita before now. Even if it was just a phone call or a postcard. Wouldn't he?"

"I'd like to think he would. But maybe he wasn't like that."

Savannah's sigh was audible. "Maybe not. We should keep trying to find him, though. It's the least we can do for Miss Rita."

Several hours later, her eyes ached, her head throbbed, she was exhausted, and Jillian still had no idea where Miss Rita's son could be. She hoped Savannah and James had had better luck, but somehow she doubted it.

Hunter Greyson picked Jillian up early Saturday morning. Blue-eyed Hunter, with strands of gray coursing through his thick dark hair, was the charming and handsome owner of Greyson & Sons Funeral Home, the only mortician in Moss Hollow. He and Jillian had been dating exclusively for a while, and it was going well.

They drove to Ballard's Milk Parlor, a small renovated house on a dairy farm a few miles out of town. Decked out in red-checked curtains and tablecloths complemented by other vintage farm decor, and only open in the mornings between six and eleven, the little café had been in business just a few weeks. A big country breakfast was their specialty, and their hearty menu was the talk of Moss Hollow.

Hunter and Jillian enjoyed thick wedges of hickory-smoked ham, cheese grits, fluffy biscuits, and creamy gravy made spicy with pork sausage and plenty of black pepper.

"If we ate here more than once a week," Hunter said, "I'd outgrow all my suits."

Jillian laughed at the idea of a chubby Hunter. Whether he wore a suit, like he did at work, or a T-shirt and jeans, as he did that day, a few extra pounds would not mar his good looks. Besides, it was the man he was on the inside that had captured her heart. "I'll take you any size or shape," she said with a smile.

"Likewise." He glanced at his watch. "What time are we supposed to be at Miss Rita's?"

"Savannah said ten-ish."

"We've got half an hour, plenty of time for a second cup of coffee. Who else is coming?"

"Besides James, I'm not really sure. Some other guys who know about cars is all I heard."

"I'm surprised you don't know more."

Jillian shrugged. "I think Savannah is keeping information about the Riviera pretty quiet, especially about what's happening today. She just wants to find out what needs to be done to restore it without much fuss. We don't want a lot of lookie-loos bothering Miss Rita, trying to buy it from her or wanting to see it up close."

"That's understandable, especially as she's so ill." Hunter sipped his coffee.

"Right. If people are going to call on her, they need to call on her because they care about her and want to make her comfortable and at peace, not needle her about that car."

"Don't you think most folks will understand that?"

"I hope so." Jillian drained her cup. "Boone Hackett will probably be there. He's the evening produce manager at Food for Less, so I imagine he'll be available. He and Miss Rita are extremely close. And Larry Don Benning is supposed to show up. Savannah said Miss Rita mentioned him the other day as the one she recommends to work on the car."

"Larry Don lives just a couple of blocks from Miss Rita, doesn't he?"

"He does."

Hunter squinted at her. "What's that face all about?"

She relaxed her features immediately. "I didn't realize I was making a face. Sorry."

"It was like you smelled something rotten. Why?"

"It's nothing, really. Well, maybe it is. I don't know."

"Jillian."

She leaned a bit toward him and spoke in an undertone. "Larry Don."

He raised one brow. "What about him?"

"He's just—oh, I don't know. I'd never have him work on my car."

"Doesn't he do a good job?"

"He's just . . ." She waved one hand dismissively and sat straight. "He's kinda creepy. Acts friendly, like he's interested in you as a person, but he always seems to have something more on his mind."

"I can't picture Larry Don flirting." Hunter's face took on hint of confusion.

"No, not that. More like he's looking for ways to take your money. Greedy."

"Oh. I see. But Miss Rita wants him to work on the car?"

She nodded.

"You're afraid he'll take advantage of her?"

"Yes."

"If she wants him to do the job, she obviously has her reasons. I wouldn't worry about it too much. Just keep an eye on what's happening and make sure he doesn't do anything that isn't on the up and up."

"I know James will be checking on the work. He's pretty savvy about cars."

"Good." Hunter shifted in his chair and cleared his throat. A frown flickered over his features. "And now I have to tell you something."

"Oh?"

"Yeah. This upcoming trip to Mobile."

"Aren't you eager to see your friends?"

"Oh, sure. It's been a few years, and I know we'll have a good time. They've got plenty of activities planned."

An unspoken "However" hung in the air, and Hunter's sudden restiveness made her uneasy.

"Go on."

"Well, my bags are packed and in the trunk of the car. I'm ready to head out this afternoon, but . . ."

Jillian curled her hands in her lap, wondering what was causing his hesitation.

"It's like this, Jillian: I'm not entirely happy about leaving."

"But why? You've been planning this trip for months now. A week's vacation fishing, hanging out, and catching up on old times. It'll be great."

"The thing is, I don't want to leave you." He made puppy-dog eyes at her that weren't serious, but weren't entirely put-on either.

Jillian returned his moony face. "You don't?"

"I absolutely do not. I'm going to miss you like crazy."

"I'll miss you too, Hunter." She reached out a hand and he grasped it. "You'll be careful driving, won't you?"

"I will. And you will take care of yourself while I'm gone?"

"You know I will."

"It'll only be a week," he said, as if reminding himself.

"Only a week."

"Less than a week, really. I'll be back next Saturday."

She nodded. Until they had this conversation, she hadn't allowed herself to think about him being gone to Alabama. For the next seven days, he wouldn't come into the bakery every day or drop by Belle Haven in the evenings. She felt a little heartsick and lonely already, but she put on a brave face and said, "As long as you can get cell phone service somewhere in the state of Alabama, we'll be just fine."

As Hunter drove them to Miss Rita's house after breakfast, each lost in private thoughts, Jillian replayed their conversation in her mind. She hated for him not to fully enjoy his vacation because he'd be missing her, but a part of her was flattered. Truth be told, she'd probably miss him more than he'd miss her. After all, she wasn't going to be around old friends, having a high time.

Jillian brushed away her thoughts as they pulled into the driveway. The front door opened and Miss Rita stepped out onto the porch, followed a few seconds later by Savannah and James. James tugged a billed cap over his balding head and raised one hand to greet them as Hunter turned off the engine. The trio paused at the bottom of the porch steps, waiting for Jillian and Hunter.

"Good morning," Jillian called as she stepped from the car. "That blouse is lovely on you, Miss Rita."

The woman gave her a smile as they walked toward her. She played with the pink-striped collar. "You know how it is when you have gentlemen callers. You want to look your best." She winked at the two men, then laughed as she linked both her arms with theirs. "Come, gentlemen. Let's go check out Savannah's new car."

"Jillian, do you have your phone?" Savannah asked. "Mine is on the charger, and James left his at home. Can you take some pictures for me?"

"Sure." Jillian took out her cell phone and pulled up the camera to have it at the ready.

Savannah hurried ahead with the key, and unlocked and opened the shed doors. She stepped to one side as the rest of the group reached the building.

Miss Rita stopped a few feet away. "I had Boone take the boards off the windows so y'all would have more light while you work." She let go of their arms and gave them both a little push. "Go ahead. See what you think."

"I think I like what I see," Hunter said with a grin. "Come on, James."

A car pulled up behind them just then, but the men were too enthralled to notice it. Jillian glanced over her shoulder in time to see Goodman "Gooder" Jones, a sheriff's deputy and frequent pain in Jillian's neck, unfold himself from the front seat of the cruiser. He approached the Buick almost reverently.

"Look at that silly man," Savannah said with a nod at Gooder. "Like he's lost his senses."

"Hey, deputy, what's on your mind?" James grinned and nudged Hunter.

"I think he's in love," Hunter said.

Gooder wordlessly bypassed everyone and entered the grimy, sunlit shed. He was so enthralled he didn't even notice when Jillian took a picture of him.

"That's the way my Ryan stared at the car when he got home," Miss Rita said. "Dumbstruck. Of course, he got over it soon enough."

Behind Gooder's cruiser, another police car showed up. Lanky Deputy Tom Shaw got out of the driver's side, and a few moments later, the passenger door opened and Sheriff Coy Henderson emerged. He stood with his hand on the open door, staring toward the shed as if expecting a sudden burst of criminal activity.

Jillian and Savannah stared at each other. Why had law enforcement shown up?

"Why's the sheriff here?" Jillian clutched Savannah's arm.

"Should we ask him?"

Jillian blinked at her. "Are you kidding? You know he'd rather get his teeth pulled without a numbing agent than to tell anyone police business."

"So why waste energy worrying?"

"I'm not worrying. Well, not exactly. It's just that when I see a cruiser . . ." She grimaced.

"You think the worst. So do I. In fact, I figure most people do. But his face!" Savannah giggled. "He's actually grinning. Take a photo of that, Jillian, because it happens so seldom this has to be a red-letter day."

Another car arrived and parked at the curb. Jillian recognized the driver, but she was still confused as to why he was there. "Hugh Honeycutt? What's he doing here? I know Miss Rita didn't send invitations or take out an ad in the *Moss Hollow Chronicle*, but it sure seems like it."

A deep frown marred Savannah's face. "No, she most certainly did not."

"Stewie Franks is probably engrossed reading the Atlanta paper in the bakery or else he'd be here too." Jillian took a photo of the gathering crowd.

"My goodness." Savannah sent an uneasy glance toward the elderly woman. "I'm sure she neither wanted nor expected this."

Sure enough, Miss Rita stood to one side, her hands curled to her chest, dismay on her face. Jillian and Savannah hurried to her.

"Did you invite them, Savannah?" the older woman asked.

"No ma'am. I'd never do something like that unless you had asked me to."

Miss Rita glanced at Jillian, who shook her head. "I didn't say a word to any of them either."

The woman sighed and gazed sorrowfully at the crowd of men gathering in the shed. "I don't know how they knew to come here this morning."

Jillian traded a glance with Savannah. Moss Hollow had a well-oiled gossip mill. No wonder a crowd had gathered for an inspection of the collector car.

"I'll go tell them to leave right now." Savannah took a step, but Miss Rita caught her arm.

"That won't be necessary. They're just here to admire a classic car. They were bound to show up sooner or later, you know. At this point, I see no reason to stop the inevitable." She turned her gaze to the men as two more joined the throng. "There's Larry Don Benning and Boone now. Larry Don's the one you'll want for some of the work."

Savannah nodded. "Yes, so you said."

"He's a good mechanic. He worked on my car when I still had it."

"Yes ma'am."

"Is Boone good at working on cars too?" Jillian took a photo of him as Miss Rita fixed her eyes on the stocky white-haired man who had yet to give the least hint of a smile.

"Boone treasures old things and old ways," she said softly. "His house is just like it was when he was growing up: same furniture, same wood paneling on the walls, same avocado-green fixtures in the kitchen and bathroom. He keeps it all shining like new."

Jillian recalled Miss Rita saying Boone had helped her to choose the Buick, and how it was his dream car. If he was as fastidious a caretaker as she implied, then surely he would have wanted a hand in keeping it in running condition. Had he been one of those who'd asked Miss Rita to sell him the car long ago?

Laughter and male voices filled the small shed as the women joined them.

"Miss Rita, ma'am." Coy Henderson doffed his sheriff's hat and gave her one of his rare smiles. "How are you this morning?"

"I'm doing better than you might think." She scanned the small crowd. "Well, fellas, what do y'all think of that beauty?"

"Why, it's mighty fine, ma'am," the sheriff said. "I remember when it was new."

Jillian took pictures of the car from several angles while everyone else chatted about it.

"It still looks new." Hunter ran a hand over the smooth red hood. "It even feels new."

"It sure does," Boone said softly.

"Yeah, on the outside." James had cupped his hands over his eyes and was peering through a window at the car's interior. "But that upholstery is shot."

"The motor is what's important. Reckon it'll run?" Hugh glanced at Larry Don Benning.

Larry Don shrugged. "Guess we'll find out when we open it up."

Sheriff Henderson took his usual position of authority and dipped his head toward the hood of the Riviera. "Then let's see what we got. Tom. Larry Don."

It never occurred to Jillian that either Deputy Shaw or Larry Don—or anyone else for that matter—would hesitate a moment to follow the sheriff's order, even when it wasn't in line of business. The men clustered around the front of the car, as eager as schoolboys at a candy counter.

Larry Don raised the hood, and the men scrambled for the best view of the engine. All Jillian could see was dirt and rust coating the parts because the men's bodies blocked her view of anything more. She didn't even bother trying to take a photo of the motor.

"It's a little crowded up here," Savannah said. "Let's check out the interior, Jillian."

They worked their way past the throng of men, Savannah going to the driver's side and Jillian to the passenger's. They opened both of the coupe's doors at the same time, and a malodorous rush of air rose to assault them.

"Phew!" Jillian reared back and waved her hand in a futile attempt to clear the stench.

"Oh my." Sadness lay heavy in Savannah's voice. "Just think what this gorgeous white leather was like before the rats and mice got hold of it."

Sure enough, both seats had huge holes and all the trim bore ragged edges from being gnawed. The red carpet had been reduced to a webby mess. Rodent droppings lay thick across every surface. Jillian took photos of it all.

"The vermin have chewed up the wiring too," Hunter said just behind Jillian. She straightened and took a step back so he could peer inside. "They did a number on these seats, didn't they?"

"It's awful," Jillian agreed.

"Sure enough, but we can replace wiring and repair engine damage," James added, peering across Savannah's shoulder. "Honey, you'll have to get the seats redone by a professional."

Savannah nodded, biting her lower lip. "Think the springs are still in good shape?"

"I wouldn't be surprised," James said. "They haven't been exposed to weather, and rats can't gnaw through metal. You'll still need padding and upholstery though."

"I know," she muttered.

The two couples eyed the damage for a little while longer, then James said, "Let's see the trunk."

"Not to be a downer, but I doubt it will be any better," Hunter said.

"I'm sure you're right." James ran his hand along the curved lines of the car and rested his palm on the trunk. "The year this car was built was the last year the company included this big of a boattail deck lid."

"That's a shame. It's a beautiful feature," Jillian said. "I love how it seems to flow from the window to the trunk, like water."

"I agree with you, but back when this car was designed, people were starting to want sleeker lines and smaller bodies, something that got better gas mileage." James unlocked the trunk and opened it.

Jillian and Savannah let out twin gasps of shock at the sight.

"Why did I even dare to hope it might be in better shape than the rest of the car?" Savannah asked. "It's completely demolished, as if something lived in here." She shuddered. "And it smells like something died here too."

"Don't lose heart." James put an arm around his fiancée. "You have a team of fellas here who love old cars and will deem it pure joy to restore this beauty. And I'll be happy to find replacement seats, if you want me to."

"That's sweet of you, but I'd love to do some of the work myself." She sighed. "Granted, I wouldn't know where to begin."

"I'd start by cleaning it all out," Tom said, peering over their shoulders at the mess. His tall body cast a shadow in the trunk's recesses. "But wear a dust mask."

"Thanks for the tip," Savannah said. "I'll be sure to do that."

"You should do that on the engine too," Gooder said to James. "Vermin have been all over every inch of it."

James nodded.

"I'll see that he does," Savannah said with a smile. She gave him a little peck on the cheek and winked.

"Anything for you, dear," he said.

"Aww." She wrinkled her nose and batted her eyelashes. "My hero."

"Good grief." Tom rolled his eyes and went back to the front of the car. As he left, the shadow he'd cast disappeared and the sunlight caught a small dark corner of something inside the trunk Jillian hadn't seen before.

"Look," she said, leaning a few inches into the trunk and taking a photo. "What's that square shape in the upholstery next to the spare tire? I don't know anything about these old cars, but I don't think it belongs there."

Hunter leaned past her, squinting hard. "You're right."

"What's got your attention back here?" Gooder said, joining them.

"That." Jillian pointed.

"Hmm." He stared hard, then unholstered his nightstick. He poked the object with it a couple of times, then reached in and ripped back the carpet. The larger hole he created revealed an oblong metal box about eight inches by twelve inches. "Get a good picture of this, Jillian. Get several."

Jillian gaped at it. "What in the world?"

Sheriff Henderson stepped away from the group of men gawking at the engine. The man always seemed to have a sixth sense, a way of knowing when something was shady, questionable, or off-kilter.

"What's going on?" he demanded gruffly. He eyed the lockbox now in Gooder's arms and, without a word, held out a hand. Gooder gave it over, and, knowing the deputy, Jillian figured he relinquished it with great reluctance. But no one argued with Coy Henderson and won.

"Where'd this come from?" the sheriff asked as he examined the box.

Gooder pointed to the gaping hole in the back of the trunk. "The springs were cut out of the back seat to make room for it."

Henderson eyed the hole but said nothing.

"Why would there be a lockbox hidden in the back seat?" Jillian asked as she took a photograph of the ruined upholstery.

"Obviously someone had something to hide." Gooder delivered this unnecessary observation with a straight face.

"There's no reason to be smart, Jones."

"I'm not being smart, sir. It's a perfectly logical assumption." He leaned in and felt around in the hole. "No key." He straightened. "Should I open it, sir?"

The sheriff dipped his head toward Savannah and handed her the box. "Ask the owner. It's hers."

Savannah bit her lip. "Do you think Miss Rita knew about this? Maybe we should ask her."

"She went back to the house a little bit ago," Hunter said.

"Oh? I didn't see her leave. She probably isn't feeling well. I'll go check on her."

Trust Savannah to shove curiosity aside when someone might need her. "I'll go with you," Jillian offered. "Do you want more pictures?"

Savannah shook her head. "We have plenty now, I'm sure."

"Are you taking that box?" Gooder asked.

"I am," Savannah said. "Miss Rita should have it."

Jillian and Savannah found the elderly woman sitting on her porch swing.

"Miss Rita?" Jillian said softly, sinking onto the swing next to her. "Are you all right?"

Silent tears streamed down Miss Rita's wrinkled cheeks, streaking her face powder. "I didn't realize . . ." She dabbed her eyes with the kind of handkerchief Jillian never saw in stores anymore. It was made from a soft floral print in shades of lavender, green, and blue, and edged with white lace.

"Didn't realize what, ma'am?" Jillian asked.

"That his car would be destroyed like that," Miss Rita replied, her watery gaze fixed on the shed. "Somehow I thought it would be exactly the same as the day I covered it with that tarp."

Savannah sank to her knees near the woman and put the box aside. "It isn't destroyed. Not really. The guys seem to think they can have it running once they clean out the engine and replace what the rodents chewed up."

Miss Rita waved her hankie back and forth in front of her face as if shooing away gnats. "I saw the interior. It's completely ruined. And oh, it was so beautiful when Ryan was here."

She blotted her tears again, wiped her cheeks, and blew her nose. The pallor beneath her powder alarmed Jillian.

"I'll go get you some water." Savannah got up and hurried into the house. Jillian caught sight of her friend's tears and hoped Miss Rita hadn't.

"Please don't upset yourself." Jillian reached over and held one of the woman's small, chilly hands.

Miss Rita stared across the yard, then brought her gaze to Jillian's face. "Did I do the wrong thing, letting that car sit there all this time? Should I have sold it right away? Maybe I should have given it to Boone, after all."

After all? Jillian had thought he'd wanted to buy it. Had he asked her just to give it to him? Jillian yearned to ask for clarification, but the poor woman was upset enough without anyone probing for information that was no one's business but her own.

"You did nothing wrong," Jillian said gently.

"I was keeping Ryan's car safe for him."

"Yes, you were."

"But—"

"Please don't dwell on it, Miss Rita. Second-guessing yourself will only make you feel worse." She gave the trembling fingers a gentle squeeze. "Besides, with all the eager hands ready to work on that car, it'll be like new again in no time. And those men will have the time of their lives doing it."

"That's right," Savannah said as she returned with a glass of ice water. "Here, drink some of this, and then I think you should go lie down for a while."

"I think this morning has been a little much." Jillian kept her voice light and caring. "With so many unexpected visitors showing up, it's bound to be a strain. Why don't we all go inside for a while?"

Miss Rita shook her head. "I'm not an invalid. Not yet, anyway. I intend to stay right here." She sipped her water. "And if you'll sit back and relax, Jillian, I can get this swing in motion."

Jillian did as requested, and Miss Rita pushed her foot against the porch floor. The swing rocked gently. Miss Rita cradled her glass in one hand and silently regarded it for a minute.

"Savannah, please go get James and Larry Don."

"Yes ma'am." Savannah scurried away.

As soon as she was gone, Miss Rita said quietly, almost as if to herself, "I have about four weeks left, if that."

Jillian caught her breath. The woman raised her eyes and stared out across her yard, her gaze moving from object to object as though memorizing every movement, every hue, every shadow. Yet Jillian still got the impression the older woman wasn't really seeing any of it.

"In the mornings, as soon as I wake up, I can tell I'm a little weaker, a little more tired. But I've never been one to give up and roll over. I won't die before my time, I can promise you that."

"Yes ma'am. Is there anything I can—"

"I'm not letting this foolish illness stop me." Rita stiffened and gave Jillian a defiant glare. "It pushes me, and I push back. I'll keep pushing back to my last breath. You see if I don't."

Jillian's admiration for the woman strengthened. "I believe you."

"Good. You should."

Savannah and the two men she'd been sent to fetch walked across the yard to the front porch. Gooder strode behind them as if he had also been summoned.

"What do you think about that car, Larry Don?" Miss Rita asked as they stepped onto the porch.

He grinned. "I think it's right sweet."

"But what about it sitting in that shed all this time? Isn't it ruined?"

"Ruined? No ma'am. I mean, some of it is ruined, like the upholstery and carpet and the tires, but that can all be replaced. And the wiring too. Relatively speaking, she's in good shape. And it'll be as near to cherry as possible when we get through working on it."

Rita's face took on an inquisitive expression. "What's that mean? Cherry?"

"Superclean, parts restored. From the frame to the taillights, all of it like brand-new."

"Is that possible?" She peered over the tops of her glasses at him. "Yes ma'am."

"She's the right color for cherry." James glanced back at the shed for a moment before turning to Miss Rita. "The paint is still like new."

"Good." Rita nodded once firmly. "Now, I want to make sure you two understand something. I've already talked to Boone, and he's going to make sure you do what I say."

A frown quickly replaced Larry Don's grin. Rumor had it that the two men didn't always get along. "Yes ma'am. What is it?"

"The Riviera is, or was, a beautiful vehicle. Even after y'all restore it, repair it, and do everything that's needed, it will still be an antique. And old things break down, no matter how well they are tended."

"Yes ma'am." Larry Don and James exchanged a glance as they said the words in unison.

Jillian wondered if everyone on that porch was considering the same thing she was: Miss Rita's body was breaking down and dying, bit by bit. Surely that's what the woman was thinking about herself.

"Here's what's on my mind," Miss Rita continued. "I want you two to make sure Savannah knows how to maintain that car—changing the oil, fixing flat tires, checking the fluids, all that kind of thing. I do not want her to be dependent on having some man take care of it for her."

"Miss Rita!" Savannah protested, blushing.

"Don't act so outraged, dear. Do you know how to change the oil? Can you change a tire?"

"I know how to check the fluid levels and the pressure in the tires. And I take my car regularly to have the oil changed."

"That's fine. But you need to know more. You men let her help on some of that engine work you'll be doing."

"I'm not—" Savannah sputtered.

"Who's a princess now?" Jillian teased.

"And teach Jillian too," Miss Rita said, eyeing her over the top of her glasses.

"Me?" Light laughter pushed back some of the somber mood. Jillian held up both hands in surrender. "Okay, all right. Teach me about cars. But I'm not crawling around in it or under it until all the rodent mess is cleaned up. If that makes me a princess, bring on the tiara."

"Make that two tiaras," Savannah added.

Much to Jillian's relief, some of the color returned to Miss Rita's face, and her mouth relaxed.

"What do you think about that box?" Gooder asked. "Is it familiar?"

"What box?" Miss Rita asked.

"The box we found in the car." He frowned at Savannah, his forehead creasing. "I thought you were going to show it to her."

"What is the boy talking about?" Miss Rita asked Savannah.

Savannah narrowed her eyes at Gooder, then returned her attention to Miss Rita. "I'll show you, ma'am." She picked up the lockbox.

"Where'd you find that?" Miss Rita gave it a suspicious once-over.

"It was hidden in the back seat of the car."

Miss Rita blinked at it. "What do you mean? It was a long time ago, but I don't remember seeing anything on the back seat the last time I looked in Ryan's car. And I wouldn't have left a box lying there."

"It wasn't on the back seat," Savannah said. "It was inside it, put in from the trunk. Someone had slit the upholstery, removed the padding, cut the springs, and stuffed this inside."

Miss Rita's mouth flew open. "Why, I declare! Who'd do such a thing? Let me see that."

Savannah handed it to her. The box presented a curiosity to everyone, and the front porch discussion brought most of the men out of the shed and away from the car to congregate near the house, curious as a bunch of cats. Boone stood a little apart, his eyes on Miss Rita as if waiting for her to speak to him.

No one said a word while she examined the box, rotating it this way and that, studying it from every angle, and poking at the lock. She shook it and something rattled against the metal.

"Here, honey," she said to Jillian. "Get some pictures of this thing."

"Do you recognize it?" Gooder asked while Jillian took several photos of it.

Miss Rita frowned, scrutinized it again, then finally sighed and shook her head. "I might be old and sick, but I have a good memory. This thing does not ring any bells with me. Boone, do you recognize it?"

He took a step forward. "No ma'am."

"It surely wasn't Ryan's. He'd never cut into his car to hide something. He loved it too much. And I know it isn't mine. Here, honey." She handed it back to Savannah. "Who has the key?"

"There wasn't one," Savannah said. "At least we didn't find one. Gooder even rooted around in the seat stuffing."

"Then how are we going to open it?" Jillian asked.

"Let me see what I can do," James said, reaching for the lockbox.

"I'll open it." Gooder grabbed it before James could.

"I'll do it." Sheriff Henderson took it out of Gooder's hands, and Jillian had to bite her knuckle to keep from chuckling.

The sheriff pulled a thin instrument from his shirt pocket and inserted it into the lock. He gave it a couple of deft turns. Everyone pressed close, their interest keen. He opened the lid.

"What on earth?" Larry Don yelped.

6

"You men move aside right now." Miss Rita's words seemed to echo from forty years ago, strong and commanding, a teacher's voice in every syllable.

The men stepped away like scolded little boys to make a path for her. She grabbed Jillian's left hand and Savannah's right and pulled them along with her.

"Let me see what's in that box, Coy Henderson."

He lowered it until all three women were able to peer at the contents.

Savannah pressed the fingers of her free hand to her lips. "Oh my goodness."

Jillian found no words as she gaped at stacks of bound money, a string of pearls, and something jeweled that glittered in the sunlight. She shook herself out of her astonishment long enough to snap a couple of photos.

"How on earth . . . ?" Miss Rita's eyes were wide as she lifted her gaze to the sheriff.

He plucked out the pearls and held their shimmering beauty to the sun. "Are these yours, ma'am?"

She gazed at them in complete astonishment. "I've never owned a string of pearls in my life. Are they real?"

"I think so," Larry Don said, although Jillian figured he wouldn't know real from faux. "How much money is that?"

Hugh moved to the front of the group. "My mama told me a trick about pearls once. If you'll allow me, Sheriff." Henderson handed him the necklace, and he studied the pearls carefully. He rubbed one against a front tooth. "It's real. A real one feels a little gritty against the tooth. A faux one will feel smooth." He passed the strand back to the sheriff.

"What's that shining?" Larry Don asked. "Diamonds?"

Savannah reached into the box and pulled out a large necklace heavy with bright stones in a gold setting.

"Now that could knock your eyes out," Hunter said.

"I'll say." Jillian took a photo. "Who'd want to wear something that flashy?"

Hunter shrugged. "Some people like showy pieces of jewelry."

"Are those real diamonds and rubies?" Larry Don gawked so intensely that Jillian thought he might give himself a headache.

Ignoring Larry Don's question, Savannah held up a silver necklace that had a small, round pendant with a brilliant center sapphire surrounded by tiny diamonds. "This is quite lovely."

"Okay if I count that money?" Larry Don asked.

"I'll count it." Gooder took out the bills. The ancient rubber bands that had bound them in stacks fell apart at his touch. Quickly he counted, lips moving silently. When he finished, he put the cash back into the box and announced, "$2,200, mostly in fifties and twenties."

Larry Don's eager expression changed to one of disappointment. "Sure looks like a lot more, doesn't it?"

Henderson turned away as if to leave.

"Are we taking the box, Sheriff?" Gooder asked.

"Nope."

"But it could be stolen goods."

"No one has reported anything stolen like that in my memory, and if it's been in that back seat all this while, the statute of limitations on it ran out a long time ago."

"But don't you—"

"The box and its contents belong to the owner."

"But—"

"Y'all have a good day, hear?" With those words, he summoned Deputy Shaw and left.

"Well, Miss Rita," Larry Don said, "looks like you've got yourself some money and some bling."

The woman had resumed her place on the swing and now she fixed a curious gaze on him.

"I have no need for some money and some—what did you call it?—bling. And even if I did, that box does not belong to me. It's Savannah's."

"Oh, but Miss Rita," Savannah cried. "That money could help pay for treatments—"

"Nonsense. There is no cure, and as I've told you before, the treatments might prolong my life a few days or a few weeks at best. No, I've had a long life, and I prefer to go the way of all living things naturally and still feeling like myself."

The others exchanged glances, but what could any of them say? It was her life and her decision.

"Take that box and find out where it came from," Miss Rita said. "Once the mystery of its origins is explained, then do with the contents as you please. And don't even think about using that money to pay for my funeral because it's all been taken care of. Boone, honey, you have the paperwork for that, don't you?"

"Yes ma'am. It's in the safe-deposit box at the bank with all the papers, just like you wanted." His normally ruddy face had lost much of its color. In fact, everyone in the group on the porch seemed wan and uneasy.

Perhaps Miss Rita noticed their discomfort, or maybe she was giving in to her ill health. Whatever the reason, she held out one hand to Savannah and said, "Help me to my room now, would you? I need to lie down for a while."

"I think I'll head on back to the shed," Hugh said. "Larry

Don, are you coming?" With a nod from Larry Don, the two men ambled to the shed.

Gooder frowned at the front door as Savannah led Miss Rita inside.

"What's wrong with you?" Jillian asked him.

He transferred the steely glare to her. "Why would you ask that?"

"You're acting like someone just stole your Easter basket."

The scowl cleared but he remained somber. "I don't like this situation, that's all."

"Who does?" Jillian sighed. "We all love Miss Rita, and she's going to be missed terribly by a lot of people."

He made an impatient gesture with one hand. "I don't mean that. I mean I don't like this business about the lockbox."

"Oh. I guess it is rather strange, isn't it?"

Gooder nodded. "You got that right. Where'd it come from? Who hid it, and when?"

"You don't think the sheriff is taking it seriously enough?" James asked.

"No, I don't."

"I bet he is," Jillian said. "You know Henderson. He spends words like they cost a fortune. He's got some ideas, but he's not sharing them with anyone."

"Including his own staff." Gooder kicked at the ground underfoot.

James cleared his throat. "You ought to be used to that by now."

"Yeah, well, this time . . ." Gooder let his voice trail into nothing.

"Don't go off on your own, Gooder," Hunter cautioned. "It will come back to haunt you."

The deputy favored him with a look that was less than appreciative before stalking away toward the shed.

"Stepped on his toes a little, didn't I?" Hunter said.

"You could say that," Jillian said, "but sometimes Gooder

needs a toe or two stepped on. He sure doesn't seem to mind stepping on mine pretty often."

"Only when you're sticking your nose into one of his investigations," Hunter told her.

"That's not the point," she replied in her haughtiest tone.

"Gooder will get over it," James said. "I've heard he has his eye on the sheriff's job."

"Coy isn't ready to hand over the reins just yet," Boone said. He'd been standing a few steps away during the entire exchange, listening silently. He, too, was a quiet man, though Jillian doubted his still waters ran as deep as the sheriff's. He'd been at his job at Food for Less longer than the sheriff had been in office, but being night manager of the produce department hardly required the deductive reasoning needed for law enforcement leadership or running a department of diverse personalities. And yet Jillian sensed in Boone a deep intelligence and a quiet strength of character. He had long been devoted to the elderly woman inside the house.

"Boone, are you sure you don't remember ever seeing that lockbox?" Jillian asked.

He held her gaze for a few seconds. "No. Why would I?"

"You've lived near Miss Rita all these years, and you knew Ryan." She shrugged. "I thought you might know something about it."

"No, I don't. She kept that shed locked up and sealed tight once that fellow from Jesup all but insisted she sell it to him. Even after she told him the car belonged to her son and she was expecting him to return any time, he called her repeatedly. Now, whether she actually expected Ryan to come home again is anyone's guess. He wasn't the good son she deserved." Boone broke off and stared across the lawn at nothing, as if he'd said far more than he'd meant to.

Jillian's mind worked fast. "Do you think that man might

have stashed the box in the car, and that's why he was so eager to have it?"

"I don't know. Maybe."

"Do you remember his name?"

"Nah. It was a long time ago."

"Do you remember anything about him? Anything at all?"

Boone rubbed his jaw, thinking. "He was middle-aged. Heavyset. If he's still alive, he'd be about Miss Rita's age. He's probably dead and gone by now."

"It's possible. But I suppose if he knew about the box and wanted to get to it, he'd have broken into the shed long before now."

"There would have been plenty of opportunities to do that over the years," James said. "Miss Rita was a busy woman back then, and she was gone from the house quite a bit."

Savannah came outside, a frown pulling her brows together. "Miss Rita would like it if everyone goes home now."

"Is she feeling worse?" Boone's face creased in concern.

"She said she's tired and doesn't want any more excitement and noise today."

"That's understandable," Hunter said. "Is there anything we can do before we leave?"

"Not that I know of, but thanks for asking. She said she's going to hire someone to clean the debris out of the shed in the next day or two, and have Larry Don haul the car to his shop so she doesn't have to deal with this kind of situation again."

"It's too much for her." Jillian sighed. "I was afraid it might be."

Savannah blinked back tears. "Yes. Too much. On many levels."

Boone broke away from the group and went into the house. Savannah started to stop him, but Jillian caught her arm.

"Let him talk to her for a minute. He's every bit as worried about her as you are, and they've been closer longer."

"I guess I'm being overprotective."

"That's perfectly understandable, sweetheart." James slipped an arm around her shoulders. "You are kind and caring. Just remember, others love Miss Rita too, and they will want to spend time with her when she's up to it. No one has any intention of causing further problems. We all want her last days to be as good as possible."

"I know. Thanks for the reminder, and I'll bear it in mind." Savannah smiled at him. "But she did ask that everyone go home now."

"I'll take care of that." Hunter stepped off the porch.

"I'll come with you," James said.

Jillian and Savannah said nothing while the men walked away. Savannah's smile seemed forced.

"You okay?" Jillian asked.

Savannah drew in her lips and shook her head. "No, I'm not."

Jillian pulled her to the swing, and they both sat. "Tell me."

"What's to tell? I'm not handling this well, and I don't think I'm going to get any better at it."

"You're feeling overwhelmed."

"You got that right. And I don't think Miss Rita is doing nearly as well as she wants everyone to believe." Savannah grabbed Jillian's hand. "I've never been in this situation before. What am I supposed to do?"

Savannah was always so self-assured and confident that Jillian hardly knew what to say. She thought for a moment, then said, "You're a strong woman, and you spread light to everyone around you. This situation with Miss Rita is difficult to deal with. It's heart-wrenching. I guess everyone believed she'd always be with us because she's always been so strong. To find out that she's fading from our lives gives us pause. Facing these coming weeks will take a lot of courage."

"Miss Rita is so brave about it, so accepting. But, Jillian, I'm not that compliant. In fact, I don't know if I can sustain courage that barely exists."

Jillian's heart twisted. "Of course you can. You're braver than you know. Plus, we'll sustain one another. And by 'we,' I mean all of us who love Miss Rita."

"That's a lot of people."

"Yes, it is." Jillian smiled. "And when one starts to flag, the others will be there for support. Accept that and give to Miss Rita all you can, knowing neither of you are alone."

The front door opened, and Boone hurried out, passing them without a word. He strode across the yard and down the sidewalk toward his house.

"He seemed disturbed." Jillian stared after him.

Savannah tensed. "I'm going to go see if Miss Rita's okay. Come with me."

They found the woman asleep in her bed, with soft music playing and a small fan stirring the air but not blowing its breath directly on her. Savannah was visibly relieved. Surely she wasn't afraid Boone had done something to hurt Miss Rita, was she?

"He must have put on that CD," Savannah whispered.

Jillian picked up the CD cover. "She likes Miles Davis?"

"She likes all kinds of music." Savannah examined the array of medicine bottles on the nightstand. "She probably took something to help her sleep. It's mild, though. Let's go out so we don't wake her up."

They quietly went back out on the porch.

"Savannah, do you trust Boone?" Jillian asked.

Her friend fidgeted a bit. "It isn't a matter of trust. It's just that he's so quiet all the time, like a mouse in the corner. Watchful and silent. You never know what he's thinking."

"I don't think you have anything to worry about. Bertie and Cornelia say they are like mother and son, and have been ever since Boone was young."

Savannah seemed unconvinced, but said nothing more.

Jillian vowed to keep her eyes and ears open, just in case her friend had a reason to worry.

If the lack of cars near the shed were any indication, all the men had left or were leaving by then except Hunter, James, and Larry Don. The three of them stopped midway across the lawn and chatted for a while, eyeing the roof of the house as if examining a problem along the ridgepole. Then, with Larry Don leading the way, they walked around the corner of the house, peering at the foundation.

"What are they up to?" Jillian asked.

"Beats me," Savannah said. "Probably checking to make sure everything is all right with the house, although Boone has tended to every possible leak, creak, and crack. They won't find anything wrong with Miss Rita's place."

"It's good she's had Boone nearby all these years."

Instead of responding, Savannah went to the marigolds that bloomed profusely in the flower beds and began plucking off dead blooms. "I'll water everything before I leave. She doesn't want me to stay, so I won't. But I'll be back to check on her."

The men came around the side of the house and joined Jillian and Savannah.

"Everything all right?" Jillian asked them.

"Yes, fine," Hunter said, his tense expression matching James's.

Larry Don appeared uncomfortable, even offended. He shot an uneasy glance at Savannah. "Get in touch when you're ready for me to take the car out of the shed." He gave a little nod and walked to his pickup.

"What's with him?" Jillian asked as he drove away.

"I should get you back to the bakery," Hunter said. She met his gaze and saw a message there.

"Yes, I'm sure Bertie could use my help. Savannah, call me if you need me."

"I will."

She had to walk fast to keep up with Hunter's long strides. Had something happened with Larry Don?

7

"**I**s everything all right?" Jillian asked Hunter as he opened the passenger door for her.

"I'll tell you in a minute," he said quietly.

She got in and fastened her seat belt while curiosity gnawed at her. Had the men found something wrong while walking the perimeter of Miss Rita's house?

"What happened?" she asked the moment Hunter got in. "You guys were smiling and talking one minute, and the next you acted like somebody canceled Christmas."

A deep frown had settled on his face. "How well do you know Larry Don Benning?"

"Mostly what I said earlier. He was several years ahead of me in school, so we're more like acquaintances than friends. Why? Did he do or say something?"

"Yeah." Hunter's voice was gruff. "He did."

She waited for him to continue, but he sat staring out the windshield at nothing, eyes narrowed.

"Are you going to tell me, or are you sworn to secrecy?"

Hunter held his silence for a little longer, then relaxed his clenched jaw and blew out a long noisy breath. "I don't like thinking the worst of people."

"I know that." She smiled at him and gave his forearm an affectionate squeeze. "You're a good man, tolerant and open-minded. I've always admired that about you, Hunter."

He offered a half-smile that faded as fast as it came. "Thank you for saying that, but I'm not fishing for compliments. I just want your take on Larry Don."

She shrugged. "He just seems—I don't know—oily sometimes. I've never heard anything *bad* about him other than he has an elevated fondness of money. What's this about?"

"He wanted us to check out Miss Rita's house. I thought we were seeing if it needed any immediate work done because it's older. James was of the same mind. But Larry Don started talking about demolition and renovation, updating and expanding this and that."

"Demolition? Update and expand? But why? Miss Rita doesn't need anything updated and expanded, especially now."

"Exactly. But that wasn't his point."

"Then what was?"

"He flat-out asked what we thought the place was worth, as is. And he asked if Boone was going to get the house when she died, and he wanted first crack at buying it. Then he lowered his voice as if someone was listening and asked if we thought Miss Rita might be willing to sell it to him right now. 'I bet I could get it for a song.' That's an exact quote. With a big grin on his face too."

Jillian was so confounded that words stuck in her throat for a moment. "He wants to try to buy the house from her while she's lying in bed, dying? Are you kidding me?"

"I am not. And now you see why James and I were what you might call fuming. James called him out on it. If he hadn't, I would have."

"What did James say?"

"He told Larry Don he thought his bargain-hunting idea was one of the most horrific things he'd ever heard of. And he compared him to a circling buzzard."

"Good for James. I hope Larry Don was properly embarrassed. Savannah will be fit to be tied when he tells her."

"*If* he tells her. He loves her so much that he doesn't want her to be hurt any more than necessary, especially while Miss Rita is in her final days." Hunter started the car and pulled out into the street. "*Some* people actually respect that kind of thing."

Jillian leaned back against the seat and folded her arms, glowering at the passing scenery. "Imagine. Speculating about the value of a dying woman's house. A woman who likes and respects him. I can't recall the last time I was this angry."

"I'm none too thrilled myself."

"I want to go to his shop and give him a piece of my mind right this instant, but it's probably not such a good idea to do that when I'm this upset."

"Probably not."

She fumed some more. "You think he's scheming?"

"Scheming?"

"To get other stuff that belongs to Miss Rita."

Hunter winced at her words. "I don't know. Maybe. I sure hope not."

"What about the car? Did he ask if he could buy that too?"

Hunter lifted one eyebrow. "I don't think so. Besides, it belongs to Savannah now, so he'd have to ask her, not Miss Rita."

"I can tell you right now, if he asks Savannah, she'll turn him down faster than a hot knife through butter."

"Will she?"

"You should have seen her face when Miss Rita handed her the keys. She was speechless. Miss Rita suggested she sell it because she could probably get a good price for it."

"And how did Savannah react to that?"

"She rejected the idea immediately of course, just like she will if Larry Don tries to buy it from her. She'll never get rid of that Riviera."

They pulled up in front of The Chocolate Shoppe a couple of minutes later. Jillian put a hand to her forehead. "In all this nonsense about Larry Don, I forgot about that box of money and jewelry for a minute."

Hunter laughed. "So did I. How could anyone forget about a box of money and jewels?"

"I don't know, but I wonder what Savannah will do with it."

"I'm pretty sure she'll be putting it in a safe-deposit box as soon as the bank opens Monday. Having something like that lying around the house isn't wise."

"You've got that right. Do you think everyone in town knows about it yet?"

He met her eyes. "Is Hugh married to Maudie?"

"Good point. If the story isn't all over Moss Hollow by now, it will be soon enough."

With a sigh, Hunter said, "I hate to say goodbye, but I need to get on the road. I'm going to miss you this week."

Jillian nodded and forced herself to smile. "You'll drive carefully?"

"I always do." He touched the side of her face tenderly, then leaned across the seat and kissed her. "I'll see you next Saturday. Take care of yourself."

"I will. Be safe, Hunter."

After a goodbye kiss, she got out of the car and watched him drive away, reminding herself how lucky she was to have a good man like Hunter Greyson in her life. She sighed, already missing him, and walked toward the bakery door.

"How'd it go?" Lenora asked the moment Jillian stepped inside The Chocolate Shoppe. She and Bertie sat at a small table near the register. Maggie, the countergirl, was polishing the glass of the display case with great industry, which meant business was a little slow right then.

The only customers were a teenage boy and girl in the far corner where Stewie Franks usually spent his mornings reading the paper. Their proximity to each other clearly signaled they were a couple, but rather than talking and laughing together the way one would expect, the attention of each was secured to the phones in their respective hands. Was this how they communicated, texting each other while sitting side by side?

Watching the pair and thinking such thoughts made Jillian feel like a cranky old curmudgeon. She looked away, dismissing the young people from her mind. The memory of Larry Don Benning's behavior immediately reared its ugly head.

"What's that face for? You didn't have a spat with Hunter right before he left, did you?" Lenora asked.

"No, no spat."

"You sure?" Bertie pinned a familiar sharp gaze on her.

"I'm sure. I'm just aggravated. Some people are so—oh, you know, *aggravating.*"

"But not Hunter. Right?"

"Right, Lenora. Not Hunter." She couldn't help but laugh at the woman's overdone concern.

Bertie got to her feet. "I'll get you a cup of coffee, and then you'll tell us who has you so aggravated, and why."

"I can serve myself, Bertie. Please sit down." She spoke over her shoulder as she filled a cup at the coffee station. "You would've thought Miss Rita had called a news conference, the way people showed up at her house."

Lenora sipped her coffee. "So we heard."

"I figured the news would make it back before I did."

"It did," Bertie said. "We heard the sheriff had to come and direct traffic."

"Oh, good grief." Jillian laughed. "He showed up, but not to direct traffic."

"Come over here and sit down before we get busy again." Bertie indicated the empty place at the table. "Tell us what really happened."

"Want a long john?" Lenora said. "We've still got some of the maple ones left."

"No thanks. Coffee is enough." Jillian took a drink, then began to relate the details of that morning.

"All those people showed up without invitation?" Bertie interrupted.

Jillian nodded. "They did."

Lenora pursed her lips, and the two older women exchanged knowing glances.

"I'm not one bit surprised," Bertie declared. "Moss Hollow has a news relay station better than anything you can find on the Internet."

"That's the honest truth," Jillian said. "I just wish I knew how information comes out in the first place."

"Honey, if it's not overheard, then it's made up." Lenora waved one hand airily. "Now, get on with it. The men were all clustered around gawking at that car, and then what?"

"They were enthralled, to say the least. Savannah even said Gooder was in love." She leaned toward them. "You should have seen him. He was *purdee* moony-eyed for sure."

They shared a laugh at that, and Jillian paused, hearing the echo of her words and the sound of her voice. How long had that drawl been creeping back into her speech? When had the idioms she'd heard as a child returned to her vocabulary? Was it the tradition of the Southern storyteller that now had her in its grip as she talked? To be perfectly honest with herself, she didn't hate it. It added another layer to a heritage she embraced more every day. Bertie and Lenora had been leaning forward, eagerly listening to every word she'd said so far. That was a sign of a good storyteller, wasn't it?

"Go on, honey," Bertie urged.

She continued, and when she reached the part about the hidden lockbox, Lenora's eyes grew bigger and bigger.

"Hold it, hold it, hold it," Lenora said. "Roll back there a minute. Where'd you say this lockbox was?"

"Inside the back seat with the stuffing."

"Completely hidden?"

"Completely." Jillian explained again where the box had been found and what some unknown person had done to conceal it there.

"Someone either put it there for safekeeping or to hide it," Bertie said. "But when and why?"

"And who?" Lenora added.

Both women had their eyes fastened on Jillian as if she knew the answers to all the puzzles. "That's what I want to find out," she said.

"You do that." Lenora tapped Jillian's wrist imperiously. "And don't forget to keep us filled in. You hear?"

"I hear." Complain as they did about gossip and rumors, these dear women possessed a curiosity that wasn't to be denied. Thank goodness neither Bertie nor Lenora passed on unfounded reports.

"Tell us the rest," Bertie said. "What was in that box?"

Jillian pulled out her phone, found the photos she'd taken, and scrolled through until she came to the ones of the jewelry. She passed it across the table to them.

"Well, I'll be," Bertie said.

"Is that jewelry real?" Lenora squinted hard at the screen.

"I imagine so. Why else would it be in a lockbox and hidden away all these years?"

"You said there was money too?"

Jillian nodded. "A couple thousand dollars."

"Goodness gracious." Bertie sat back.

"Is it counterfeit?"

Jillian blinked at Lenora. "I never even thought of that. Maybe. But it was old, with smaller portraits in the design. And it was wrinkled and obviously used, not crisp and uncirculated the way you'd think a stash of counterfeit money would be."

"You wouldn't know a counterfeit bill anyway, sugar." Lenora gave her a beatific smile, as if Jillian's ignorance of phony money was proof of her goodness.

"No, I wouldn't. And neither would either of you. Gooder is the one who counted it, though, and he didn't say anything."

"What did Miss Rita have to say about that box of money and jewelry?" Bertie asked.

"She's as mystified as everyone else. After a little while, she asked Savannah to have everyone leave—"

"She should've ordered them off the place when they first trooped in like a pack of dogs," Lenora said.

"That's right." Bertie nodded vigorously.

"—and she's going to have Larry Don Benning tow the car to his shop where they can work on it."

"Oh?" Bertie frowned. "I guess he'll do a good job, but he's liable to overcharge."

"His garage isn't that far from where she lives, so she's probably having him do it because he's a neighbor," Lenora added. "Miss Rita is loyal that way."

Bertie studied Jillian's face. "What's that expression for? You've been wearing it ever since you walked in here."

Lenora examined her as well. "And it's not about Hunter?"

Jillian gave an exasperated little sigh. "No, it has nothing to do with Hunter, except I'm going to miss him this next week. But that's not at all why I'm irritated."

"Well, for goodness' sake, what is it?" Bertie asked.

"I don't want to sound too much like Wanda Jean."

Lenora cleared her throat loudly and glowered at her. "Stop beating around the bush and tell us what's on your mind. I declare, Jillian, you're trying my patience."

She told them about Larry Don's interest in the worth of Miss Rita's house. "And from what Hunter said, there he was, coming up with ideas of what to knock down, build on, update, and I don't know what else. Hunter and James could tell you more, but it galls me."

"Tacky little pip-squeak." Lenora sat back and folded her arms. "How does he think he's gonna get his hands on her property anyway? I figure she'll leave it to Boone Hackett."

"Was Larry Don getting all buddy-buddy with Boone?" Bertie asked.

"Not that I noticed. The men spent most of the time drooling over that car."

"We'll need to keep an eye on that boy," Lenora said. "Tell the others."

"You think he's untrustworthy?"

Lenora harrumphed. "I don't know what I think about him. Just don't let him take advantage of that poor old woman."

"I can assure you that will not happen. Not with Savannah, James, Hunter, and me watching out for her."

Bertie beamed. "Why, Jillian, I don't know when I've been prouder to be your grandmother."

Jillian cracked a smile. "Thanks, Bertie."

Lenora got up and filled their cups. "I bet Boone will be on the lookout too. I don't think he and Larry Don have ever gotten along too well."

Jillian started to sip her coffee but stopped. "I didn't see any sign of conflict between them."

"Well, you probably wouldn't. Boone doesn't exactly wear his heart on his sleeve." Bertie tipped her head to one side, clearly pondering something. "You know what? It's been a while since I've seen Boone. Let's have him over for supper."

Jillian blinked. "You don't mean tonight, do you?"

"That's what I had in mind. I believe we can gently sound him out, find out if he's clued in to Larry Don's intentions."

"That boy isn't very social, y'know," Lenora said.

"I know, Lenora, but he's not antisocial either. Just quiet. Invite him over, Jillian."

"What about Aunt Cornelia?"

Bertie frowned. "What about her?"

"Shouldn't she be consulted before we invite guests for dinner?"

Bertie waved one hand. "You know she loves company. And I sincerely doubt Boone will want something big and fancy."

"Still, I'll call her before I get in touch with him."

"That's fine, honey. Invite Savannah while you're at it. You come too, Lenora."

"Thank you kindly," Lenora said, "but as much as I'd like to know the details of this situation, I believe the fewer people around your table tonight, the more likely Boone is to talk. I'll stay home, but you make sure I find out what's said."

Jillian considered her words. "We'd love to have you, but you could be right. Savannah and James are going to the movies, but they aren't staying out late in case Miss Rita needs something."

"So it will be just the four of us then," Bertie said. A movement outside caught their attention. "Carful of teenagers coming in," she said, getting up. "We can handle the work here, Jillian. You go call Cornelia and invite Boone." They left the table as a loud and laughing group of young people trooped inside.

In the kitchen, Jillian dialed Belle Haven. Cornelia answered after a few rings, and Jillian explained Bertie's plan to invite Boone to dinner.

"Think he likes pork roast, fried potatoes, and applesauce?" Cornelia asked. "That's what I'm fixing. And buttermilk pie for dessert."

"I guess we'll find out. Sorry to spring this on you."

"Don't be silly. It's no problem to make extra biscuits and lay another plate. Boone Hackett isn't exactly a bigwig who expects a fancy table, but I don't want to serve him food he doesn't like. You find out if he likes pork roast. If not, it'll be hamburgers. Everybody likes hamburgers."

"Thanks, Aunt Cornelia. I'll let you know if you need to change your menu."

After finding Boone in the phone book, Jillian dialed his number. When he answered, she said, "Hi, Boone. It's Jillian Green."

"Is Miss Rita okay? She was fine when I left, I swear." Panic tinged his voice.

"She's fine, Boone," Jillian said reassuringly. "I've actually called you because Bertie, Cornelia, and I would like to invite you for dinner at Belle Haven tonight."

"*Me?*" The astonishment in his voice nearly caused her phone to glow.

"Yes, you. I know it's last minute, but we'd really like it if you could join us."

"But . . . me?"

"Why are you so surprised, Boone? We've known one another for years and years."

"That's true. To be honest, though, I don't remember the last time someone invited me for supper. Besides Miss Rita, of course."

Her heart twisted a little. "Will you come?"

After a short pause, he said, "I'd be honored. Thank you."

She remembered Cornelia's words. "Pork roast okay with you?"

"Absolutely."

"We usually have dinner around six or so. Come earlier, if you'd like."

"Thank you. Thank you so much."

She smiled as she ended the call. Cornelia was glad to have

a guest, and the guest was glad to be invited. Jillian hoped the evening would hold the same warmth and grace.

She had no sooner ended the call with Boone than her cell phone rang. Caller ID told her it was Sheriff Henderson.

"E-mail me those pictures of the box's contents."

That's our sheriff, straight to the point. "Are you going to try to find out where the money and jewelry came from?" Jillian asked.

"I'm looking into it. Send me the pictures. ASAP."

"Yes, sir." She spoke to dead air, then did as he asked. It was a good thing Coy Henderson was a great sheriff and a decent man. Otherwise, she might take offense.

Boone rang the bell a few minutes before six. Jillian opened the door and blinked in surprise at what she saw. She could recall no time in her life when she had ever seen him dressed in anything other than the store uniform he wore at Food for Less. He'd even been wearing it that morning at Miss Rita's. That evening, however, he wore chinos and a white button-down shirt. His leather shoes gleamed softly. She had never noticed what lovely hair he had, thick and snowy white with a gentle wave. His icy blue eyes were fringed with heavy, dark lashes. Boone Hackett was a far more handsome man than she'd realized.

He held three items in his arms and gave her a nervous smile. "Good evening."

"Hi, Boone. Won't you come in?" She stepped back.

He walked inside, glancing around the foyer a moment before his gaze traveled upward to the multifaceted skylight in the dome three floors above them. He gazed wonderingly at it for a few seconds, then turned to Jillian. "I've brought something for each of y'all."

"That's so sweet of you," she said. "Bertie and Aunt Cornelia are putting out the food. I'll go tell them you're here."

"No need," Bertie said, coming from the dining room. "Here we are."

Both women approached, smiling. "My goodness, you brought an armful," Cornelia said.

"I did." Boone gave a half smile. "The plant is for you, ma'am, because everyone in town knows how you love to garden. Of course, this is an indoor plant. I hope that's okay."

Cornelia took the dark green philodendron from his hand, her eyes shining. "Thank you so much. I love these kinds of plants. Our mother had one growing in the corner. It grew to be so big Bertie would hide behind it when we'd have callers."

"Mercy, Cornelia. Don't tell all our family secrets," Bertie scolded. "That is a lovely plant, Boone. If we put it where our mother grew hers, it will probably get just as big."

"I hope so," Cornelia said. "Just don't you go hiding behind it when I need help in the kitchen."

Amidst the laughter, Boone held out a box of candy to Bertie. "I know you have a shop full of cakes and cookies, but these were my mama's favorite kind of candies. You were always so kind to her." He shrugged and ducked his head. "I thought you might like them."

"I love Norway fudge cremes," Bertie said with a big smile as she peeked inside the red box. "And I haven't had them for years. I didn't even realize anyone still made them."

"Yes ma'am. They still make them over in Bristow. I go over there once in a while to pick up some for Miss Rita." He glanced at the box in Bertie's hand, and his smile was wistful. "She and Mama could eat an entire box in one sitting if they weren't careful."

"Well, bless your heart. Thank you, Boone."

"You're welcome. Jillian, this is for you. I make them." He handed her a small gift bag, from which she pulled a cluster of interlocking wooden blocks, some pale oak, some dark walnut. "You're so good at putting two and two together to get to the bottom of trouble that a puzzle seemed appropriate."

"A puzzle?" She stared at the intricate structure. "Wow! You make these?"

He nodded. "A sort of hobby, you might say."

She studied the puzzle again, turning it this way and that,

admiring the smooth wood and trying to see how the pieces fit together. "I love it, but you'll have to show me how to work it."

He shook his head with what looked suspiciously like a mischievous grin. "You have to figure it out for yourself."

"She can do it," Cornelia declared. "Our Jillian is a smart cookie."

"All three of you are." He smiled. "I'm mighty honored to be invited to have supper with you."

"And we're tickled to have you, Boone," Bertie said. "Come on. Supper's on the table."

Boone was a quiet man, but well-spoken and willing to talk as they ate. Which, as it happened, was a good thing, because Cornelia peppered him with questions as soon as he sat down.

"For goodness' sake, let the boy eat before his food turns cold," Bertie said, frowning at her sister.

"All right." Cornelia ate a couple of bites, then tipped her head to one side and studied Boone's face. "You're a handsome fella, Boone."

He flushed to the tops of his ears, but said, "Thank you, ma'am."

"Why aren't you married?" she pressed.

"Cornelia! I declare, you act like you don't have any raising." Bertie turned to Boone. "I apologize for my sister."

"Oh hush, Bertie. Boone knows I don't mean any harm, don't you, dear?" She smiled at him. "So tell me, whatever happened to Janine? That was the name of that girl you were engaged to, wasn't it?"

At the mention of the name, Boone froze with the fork halfway to his lips, his eyes on the plate. His ears grew even redder. Jillian sought the words to relieve his obvious embarrassment. She had no idea how to cover this gaffe. If Cornelia had been a few years younger, she might have given her shin a kick under the table. As it was, all she could think to do was offer more food.

"Have some more applesauce, Boone. I believe Bertie bought these apples from your produce department."

He blinked at her as if he didn't understand her words, but a moment later he took in a deep breath, took the bowl, and spooned more onto his plate.

"Thank you." He glanced at Cornelia. "Janine, yes. She was from over in Bristow. We broke up a few weeks after Ryan came home."

"Oh?" Confusion clouded Cornelia's eyes. "I thought you were together at Moss Hollow's Bicentennial Celebration back in 1983, when Raymond and I came home for a visit. Remember that sister? Moss Hollow made a big to-do over the town's founding with a parade and everything." She looked at Boone again. "I thought I saw you kiss Janine at the fireworks that night."

"No ma'am. You're thinking of Regina Talley."

The clouds cleared from her eyes. "Oh, yes. I got the names mixed up. They sound a little alike, don't they? Janine, Regina. Regina, Janine."

He gave her a quick smile. "Yes ma'am, I guess they do."

"Well, whatever happened to Regina? You two were going to get married, weren't you?"

"Oh, forevermore!" Bertie said. "You don't have to answer that, Boone. Please forgive my sister. She's getting to be as nosy as Wanda Jean."

Cornelia gasped. "I most certainly am not. You take that back."

"It's okay, Miss Bertie. Miss Cornelia, Regina and I were never engaged. We weren't what you'd call compatible." He shrugged. "I'm not very social, and I like things nice and simple."

"And she didn't? She wanted to run around and have parties?" Cornelia asked.

"Something like that, yeah."

Bertie frowned at her sister, but Cornelia ignored her. "That's too bad." She gave his hand a little pat. "You're a fine man, Boone. Steady and honest. You work hard and mind your own business."

He flushed a third time and returned to his supper. "Thank you for saying so, ma'am."

"Whatever happened to those two women?"

"Regina married a preacher down in Savannah and they have a couple of kids. Maybe even grandchildren by now."

"I see."

He glanced up and favored Cornelia with a smile. "This is a mighty good meal, ma'am. It's been awhile since I've had homemade applesauce."

"Not only did we buy the apples from your produce department, Boone," Bertie said, "we used your mama's recipe."

His face lit up. "Did you? Well, it sure is fine. Better than fine."

"I'm glad you like it. I'll send some home with you, if you'd like."

"That would be nice. Thank you."

"What about Janine? Whatever happened—ouch! Who kicked me?" Cornelia reached down to rub her leg, glaring at Bertie.

"I did not kick you. I nudged you." Bertie glared back through narrowed eyes. "Now pass me the butter, if you please."

A brief silence fell over the table. Before Cornelia could continue her probing into Boone's past, Jillian took in a deep breath and said, "So, Boone, did you stop by Miss Rita's this afternoon?"

"I sure did. Right before coming here, in fact." He passed around a glance. "She said to tell y'all hello. And she says she enjoyed those cherry turnovers."

"Bless her," Bertie said.

"How was she feeling?" Jillian asked. "I know the events of this morning tuckered her out."

He nodded. "It did, and she stayed tired. She won't admit it, though." He paused and met Jillian's eyes. "This thing that has her—there's no cure for it, is there?"

He harbored such desperate hope on his face that Jillian longed to reassure him their elderly friend would conquer the disease and become whole again. But she couldn't, and she refused to offer him false hope. Even if she were to give him such a guarantee, he would not accept it, because he could see the truth for himself.

"Maybe someday there will be a cure," she said softly. "Let's hope so. But right now, there's nothing that can be done."

His face twitched a little. "Yeah, that's what I thought."

"There is a lot of information online about everything these days," Jillian said. "I'm sure you could find some articles that would help you understand more about what's happening to Miss Rita. If you want to."

"I don't have a computer." He studied his fried potatoes as if they held the secret of world peace.

"The library has public-access computers. Or I'd be happy to print out some things for you."

"No thanks." He shifted in his chair and kept his eyes down.

"If you change your mind—"

"No, Jillian." He frowned at her. "I don't read very well, so . . . no, thank you."

"Sure." She felt awkward, embarrassed, almost as if she had made a bigger blunder than Cornelia had.

Bertie cleared her throat and came to the rescue. "From what Jillian told us earlier, I understand Ryan's old car has created quite a stir of interest for some people. What do you think?"

He cocked an eyebrow. "What do you mean?"

"Jillian said it was going to need work, but she's not an expert on cars. So I was curious as to your opinion. Do you think it'll get to running again?"

"It might not need as much work as you'd think after being left untouched for so long. It's been kept out of the elements in that old shed all this time, so that's a good thing. The damage would have been a lot worse if it'd been left outside. Of course, you can't protect something from the humidity in this climate, so there's some rust. I'm sure Jillian told you about the mess the varmints made. They've done the most harm."

Cornelia shuddered. "Indeed she did."

"Rodents are so destructive," Bertie added.

"Miss Rita wants that shed cleaned out," Jillian said. "After seeing it, I don't blame her. In fact, if I were her, I think I'd just tear it down. It's not in that great of shape."

Boone shifted in his chair. "We've talked about that, but as far as I know, tearing it down has never been in her plans."

"It sounded as though she's planning to hire someone to take care of the mess right away."

"Oh, is she?" He frowned. "I told her I could do it and save her the expense of hiring it out. I wonder why she didn't say anything to me." He shrugged. "But if she wants it done right away, she probably didn't want to bother me with it. She's like that, you know. Not wanting to bother folks with her own needs."

"She has always been like that. I understand Larry Don is going to repair the car," Bertie said, eyeing him closely.

"The engine, yes."

"You think he'll do a good job?"

"As good as anyone, I reckon."

"I don't trust him." Cornelia's sudden declaration made them all stare at her.

"No?" Boone lifted one brow.

"It's a feeling I get when I'm around him. He has always seemed just a little bit too eager, too friendly, if you know what I mean. Like a snake-oil salesman. Don't you think so?"

"I understand what you're saying, ma'am. He wants to make money, and he's sly, but I don't think he's dishonest."

"You don't?"

"Nah. Just slick and, to be frank, greedy."

"So what do you think about him taking care of the Riviera?"

"He'll do an all right job, probably even a fine job. I gotta admit, though, I wish Miss Rita wasn't so set on having him do the work because he charges more than anyone else in town. But Savannah is going to do what Miss Rita wants."

"We always go to Cal Haskell," Bertie said. "He's as slow as molasses, but he gets the job done right, and he doesn't overcharge."

"Do you think Larry Don will take advantage of Savannah, Boone?" Jillian asked.

"He'll probably try."

"That's what I was afraid of." Bertie wiped her lips and folded her napkin. "Savannah is a good girl."

"Her being a 'good girl' isn't in question," Jillian said. "She doesn't want to upset Miss Rita, especially now." She laid a hand on Boone's arm. "Will you do all of us a favor? Will you keep an eye on him and make sure he doesn't do anything underhanded where Miss Rita is concerned? If she uses him just because he's a neighbor, then likely he takes advantage of her more often than we realize."

"You can bet on that, but he can't get away with much, not with the other guys who'll be there. They're all hankering for a chance to work on that car." Boone paused and sent a speculative gaze around to each of them. "Excuse me for saying this, but it seems to me more is going on here than meets the eye. Have you seen or heard something in particular that's causing you extra worry?"

"Just the way he was acting at Miss Rita's place today," Jillian said. She picked her words carefully because she didn't want to be the implement that sharpened hard feelings. "He seemed overly interested in everything."

"You mean that lockbox?"

She nodded.

"Yeah, I noticed that. I figure he might try to wangle it out of Savannah. Maybe offer to fix the car in exchange for the contents of that box."

"Do you think the value of those contents would be equal to the value of his work?"

"Hard to say, but I'm afraid if he thinks there is anything of value that Miss Rita owns, he'll try to get his hands on it."

Jillian had heard enough and was convinced Boone would keep Miss Rita's and Savannah's best interests at heart.

She and Bertie exchanged a glance, but Cornelia was gazing at Boone with speculation brewing in her blue eyes. *What is she up to?* Jillian braced herself, preparing for whatever was about to issue from her aunt's mouth.

"Do you like cats?" Cornelia asked.

He blinked, as if the abrupt change of subject had startled him.

Jillian winced. A discussion of cats was likely to edge the conversation into her great-aunt's wacky beliefs. For instance, that her dear departed Raymond communicated through Possum, the fluffy cream-and-brown cat that had shown up at Belle Haven when he was a kitten.

"I like cats," he said. "I don't have any, but there are some strays in the neighborhood, and I put out food for them."

"Then you have cats." Cornelia gave him a warm, approving smile.

"Or maybe they have you," Bertie added.

Boone chuckled. "I don't like to see an animal go hungry. It's a small enough thing to put out food for them."

"Bless your heart," the twins chorused, and Jillian warmed toward him.

How was it that they were merely acquaintances instead of good friends? Maybe it was because Boone was considerably younger than Bertie and Cornelia and considerably older than herself, and he was a reserved man, not given to pushing himself forward. Even so, he was articulate, intelligent, and genteel. Perhaps after that night, he would become a more frequent visitor at Belle Haven.

"How about some buttermilk pie?" Cornelia asked, getting up.

A big smile spread over his face. "Yes ma'am!"

A little later, after dinner plates had been cleared and while Cornelia served pie and coffee, Jillian asked, "Weren't you and Ryan Carter close friends?"

"We grew up a couple of houses apart, and we hung around together until we got into our teens."

"You weren't friends after you got older?"

"Not so much. He got restless, and running wild just wasn't my thing. After his eighteenth birthday, his number came up and he was sent to Vietnam. I spent a lot of time with Miss Rita that year, trying to help her get through his absence. That's when she and I became close."

"She said you were like a second son."

"Aw, well." He ducked his head. "My mama had died the previous year, and I needed Miss Rita as much as she needed me. I reckon you could call me a homebody, so I was close by all the time if she needed anything. I was someone she could dote on and spend time with who wouldn't abuse her kindness and generosity." He smiled at Cornelia. "Ma'am, I believe this is just about the best buttermilk pie I ever put in my mouth."

"I'm glad to hear it. You take some of it home with you, hear?"

"Yes ma'am. Thank you."

"Miss Rita has always been a good cook," Bertie said.

"She's a great cook," he said. "Or she was. She hasn't done much cooking in the last year or so."

"Maybe after all these years, she's tired of it," Jillian said. "I would be."

Cornelia scowled at her. "Why, my goodness, what a thing to say. Have I ever gotten tired of cooking? Has your grandmother ever gotten tired of making bread and doughnuts and cake?"

Sometimes Cornelia took up a challenge where none existed. Jillian kept her mouth shut.

"Miss Rita has never slowed very much until recently," Boone said. "And she sure doesn't want anyone to know that she's lost her zip. As energetic as she's been, I think maybe this sickness has been creeping up on her for a while, and she's just not given in to it."

The moment was suddenly heavy. Lost in their own thoughts, no one spoke for a time, but questions continued to writhe in Jillian's brain like worms in fertile soil.

"Do you have any idea where Ryan might be now?" she asked after a while.

"Not the least notion." He shook his head. "If I had known back then where he ran off to, I'd have gone after him. And you better believe I would've given that boy a piece of my mind, abandoning his mama like that."

"I don't blame you." Jillian toyed with her napkin. "It's hard to believe anyone could just go away and never come back when someone at home loves them so much. That is something I do *not* understand."

"Me neither, Jillian."

"Didn't anyone try to find him, though? He was considered a missing person, wasn't he?"

Boone snorted. "Nah, not Ryan. He was always threatening to leave her high and dry, especially when she couldn't give him what he wanted as soon as he wanted it. When he left, she blamed herself." He shook his head, his face filled with pain. "She didn't need him around her. He caused her all kinds of problems and grief."

"Well, he needs to be here now, before she passes," Jillian said. "If he were to come back, that would bring Miss Rita a lot of peace. Don't you think?"

"I'd like her to have peace, sure enough, but I figure if he was going to come back, he'd have done it before now."

"But why did he leave in the first place?" Jillian asked.

Boone pinned a gaze on Jillian. "Folks say Miss Rita spoiled him, but being a single woman with a kid to raise on a teacher's pay, she had limits. Ryan didn't care. Not about her, not about me, not about anyone. The plain fact is he was self-centered all his life. When he was a kid, he could sweet-talk anyone into or out of anything. And it didn't bother him in the least who he hurt or how much trouble he caused. I reckon the day he left, he woke up dissatisfied with something and took a notion to fly the coop."

"If that's what happened, it was cruel beyond words." Jillian shook her head.

"It sure was," Boone said. "Miss Rita had—and still has—a heart of gold. I was with her the day she bought him that expensive car. I don't believe I have ever seen her so excited. It was Ryan's dream car, and she couldn't wait to give it to him." He paused and a dark expression flashed across his face. "I tried to talk her out of it. I knew a fellow who had a good used Chevy for sale that would have been a sight easier on her pocketbook. It would have been just fine for Ryan, but nothing would do except that fancy red Riviera."

Was that a note of bitterness in his voice? Jillian tried to study his expression, but he stared fixedly at the last of his pie as he finished it.

"Did he ever mention some specific place he wanted to go?" she asked. "Even if we just knew a state he wanted to visit, it might be a good start to tracking him down."

He shook his head. "He never expressed any travel plans to me." He pushed away his empty plate and rested his elbows on the table. His eyes grew thoughtful. "The thing is, that stint in Vietnam seemed to have changed him for a little while. Settled him down."

"That was a bad time, back then," Cornelia said. "So many of the boys who served came back changed, and seldom for the better."

"Oh, I remember," Bertie said.

"Yes ma'am." Boone nodded. "I didn't go because I have no hearing in my left ear. Ryan stayed at home more after he got back, at least for a while, and I've never seen Miss Rita so happy. Me and Ryan even spent time together like we did when we were kids, fishing and hiking and such." He picked up his coffee cup. "Miss Cornelia, do you have more coffee made?"

"Why, sure thing." She slipped into the kitchen and returned with the pot to fill his cup. "More pie?"

"Thank you, ma'am, but no. I've had plenty." He took a drink and continued talking. "Once Sonny Stonemaker came to town, it wasn't long before Ryan took up his old ways. I wasn't surprised by anything he said or did."

"Sonny Stonemaker?" Cornelia looked at Bertie. "I don't remember him, do you?"

"Was he that boy who showed up a few weeks after Ryan came home?" Bertie asked.

"Yep. From some little town in Missouri. They served in Vietnam together. A bad egg, that one. Once he came to Moss Hollow, that was it between me and Ryan. I'd come around and check on Miss Rita, but me and Ryan—" He made a flat, slicing gesture with his hand. "And then, after a while, he up and left."

"What about Sonny?" Jillian asked.

"What about him?"

"I mean, who was he? What do you know about him?"

"Not much. He was a troublemaker with a fondness for carousing. He was older than Ryan."

"Did he stay here, or did he go back to Missouri?"

"I always figured they left together. You would've thought they'd go in Ryan's car, but Sonny had a van. You know, one of those hippie vans that some people lived in back then while they drifted around the country 'finding themselves.'"

"But if Ryan loved that car as much as Miss Rita seems to

believe he did," Jillian said, "you'd think he'd at least have come back for it, if for no other reason."

"Yeah, you'd think." Boone cradled his coffee cup between his palms, a heavy frown on his face.

"I wonder where they went." Jillian mused aloud. "And where they are now."

"Maybe they're both dead," Cornelia ventured.

"It's possible," Boone said. "I've wondered the same thing. Can't live that kind of lifestyle and expect long, healthy years to follow. I never said such a thing to Miss Rita, though, you can be sure."

"Of course not," Bertie murmured.

"I think she still believes he'll come home," Jillian said.

Boone nodded. "Some days she thinks he's going to walk through her front door, and other days, she's sure he's gone and she'll never see him again."

"That makes me want to cry." Cornelia blinked hard.

"Me too, ma'am."

"I'm not about to tell her I couldn't find anything about him online," Jillian said. "That is, nothing that matches the name Ryan Carter from Moss Hollow."

"I say let her cling to the belief he might return," Bertie said. "There's no reason to upset her now."

Jillian glanced around the table. "But wouldn't it be wonderful if we could find him before she passes away?"

Boone raised one eyebrow. "I don't know about that. On one hand, yeah, it might be great, but on the other, who knows what he's like now? He might be some kind of weathered ex-con or something. If he isn't dead, he might be in prison. The way he lived, it's pretty likely."

"You have a point," Jillian said, "but I still can't help but think that if he were incarcerated, there would be a record of it online. Don't you believe so?"

"I don't know. Maybe, maybe not." Boone seemed to be getting weary of the subject.

Cornelia stopped and peered around the room. "Has anyone seen Raymond in the last few minutes? I bet he knows where Ryan is. I doubt he ever met Sonny, so he wouldn't know him at all."

Boone slid a mystified glance at her. Cornelia's eccentricities were known in Moss Hollow but most people rarely spoke of them.

"My Raymond speaks through Possum, you know," Cornelia said to Boone.

He raised both eyebrows. "He does?"

"Oh, yes. We have some delightful conversations."

"Aunt Cornelia." Jillian shook her head slightly.

Cornelia crimped her mouth, then seemed to think again. She leaned toward Boone and whispered, "My sister and great-niece prefer I not talk about the Raymond-and-Possum connection. I'll find out what Raymond knows and tell you later."

"Yes ma'am," he answered.

She smiled and straightened.

"Boone, what do you know about Sonny?" Jillian asked.

"Not much. I haven't thought about him in years. I remember he hated the South, and he despised Moss Hollow."

"Why, forevermore!" Cornelia's posture stiffened. "What kind of person would despise Moss Hollow? It's so quiet and peaceful most of the time."

"Exactly," Boone said. "Sonny was noisy and restless. He wanted to go where the action was."

"Back then, California was a mecca for people seeking action. It still is," Jillian said.

"And aren't we so lucky it gave you back to us, dear?" Bertie said. "I'll take Moss Hollow, Georgia, any day of the week."

"Me too." Boone gave her a big smile. "No place like home, eh, Miss Bertie?"

"You got that right, honey."

"Raymond and I had to move to Atlanta because of his job, but I've never understood folks who want to leave here," Cornelia added.

The twins faced Jillian, their expressions identical.

"Don't look at me like that. I came back, didn't I? I'm staying, aren't I?"

"See that you do," Bertie sniffed. "If you were to run away from home like Ryan Carter, I don't know what we'd do."

"You have nothing to worry about, Bertie. My feet are firmly planted right here. For better or worse."

After Boone left and the supper dishes had been cleaned, Jillian excused herself and settled down on her bed with her laptop. She typed *Sonny Stonemaker* into the search engine and bit her lip. Then she released it when she found exactly nothing other than references to stonemakers as a vocation. As she had done when searching for Ryan's name, she varied the spelling but continued to find no link to the man Boone had told them about.

In an age when nearly everyone's name had a mention or a profile somewhere online, how was it she was unable to find information about either of the two men? She would have texted Savannah, but she and James were at the movie theater, and Jillian refused to interrupt her friend's evening out.

She closed her laptop and sighed as she slouched on the bed. "Remember what Scarlett said," she muttered. "'Tomorrow is another day.'"

The next morning, Jillian's phone rang just as she stepped out of the shower. She wrapped herself in a huge bath towel and ran to pluck her cell phone off the night table.

"Hey, how soon can you get to the hospital?" Savannah asked in lieu of a greeting.

Her heart stopped. "As soon as I get dressed and drive over. What's happened? Are you okay?"

"It's Miss Rita. Get here as soon as you can."

Savannah ended the call before Jillian had a chance to ask what had happened. Was Miss Rita suffering a sudden decline? Jillian figured anything was possible for someone of her advanced age with a terminal illness. She threw on a pair of jeans and a T-shirt, pulled her wayward wet hair into a ponytail, slid her feet into a pair of sandals, and ran downstairs.

"What's happening here?" Bertie asked as she came out of the kitchen in her bathrobe, a mug of coffee in her hand. "You aren't wearing that to church, are you?"

"No. I'm heading to the hospital. Savannah just called and said something about Miss Rita."

"Said what?"

"Nothing. She just mentioned her name."

Bertie stopped in her tracks. "What do you reckon is wrong?"

"She didn't say, but I'll call you as soon as I find out." She kissed her grandmother's cheek and ran out of the house.

A short time later, she found Savannah in the second-floor waiting room, absently thumbing through a battered magazine. Her friend was pale and frazzled.

"What's happened?" Jillian said, rushing toward her.

"Oh, I'm so glad to see you." Savannah jumped up and hugged her. "The doctor is with Miss Rita right now." She sent an anxious glance toward a door several yards away.

"Tell me what's going on." Jillian sat on the edge of a chair and pulled Savannah down in the one next to her. She took one of Savannah's hands in hers. It was cold and trembling. "Did she collapse or what?"

"I'm not sure what happened. All I know is she called 911 in the middle of the night but said hardly anything. When the emergency crew arrived, she was lying on the ground."

"Lying on the ground? You mean she was outside in the middle of the night?"

Savannah nodded. "Who knows how long she'd been lying there, but she was in shock by the time they arrived."

Jillian gripped the arm of the chair. "This makes me feel woozy, Savannah."

"You and me both. They've been running tests and monitoring her for a while, but no one has told me much of anything. I don't even know if she's hurt or sick or why she was outside in the first place."

"How long have you been here?"

"Not that long." Savannah glanced at the wall clock. "She was out of it when they brought her in, and they didn't know who to call. That silly confidentiality business prevented them from calling anyone without her permission, and without any family . . . Anyway, as soon as they brought her around, she asked for Boone and me."

"Boone's here?" Jillian's gaze darted around for him.

"No. They couldn't reach him. Neither could I, though I've tried a dozen times. It's been a few minutes since the last time I tried, though, so I'll give it another shot."

"Did you leave a voice mail or text him?"

Savannah gave a short, humorless laugh. "Are you kidding? Boone Hackett doesn't have a cell phone. He doesn't even have an answering machine."

"Maybe he unplugged his phone at home."

"Maybe he's out of town."

Jillian shook her head. "I doubt that. He was at Belle Haven for supper last night, and he never said a word about going anywhere. Besides, he told us he likes to stay home."

Savannah frowned at her cell phone. "Still no answer." She glanced over Jillian's shoulder and stiffened. "The door to Miss Rita's room just opened."

They got to their feet, tensely watching and waiting for someone to come out. A nurse emerged. Savannah approached the woman with Jillian a step behind.

"Excuse me, but what's happening with Miss Rita?"

The young nurse blinked at her. "Who?"

"Miss Rita. Rita Carter. She's in that room." Savannah gestured toward it.

"Oh, her."

"Yes, *her*." Savannah's usually gentle voice was sharp. "What can you tell me about her?"

"Are you a family member?"

"No, she has no—"

"Then I can't tell you anything. Excuse me."

"But I'm—"

The woman hurried away as if she were about to attend to an emergency. Another woman in scrubs came out, this one was middle-aged with gray-streaked brown hair pinned in a thick knot on the back of her head.

"Dr. Cowan." Savannah sighed. "Thank goodness."

The woman smiled at her. "Hi, Savannah. I know you've been anxious, so let me tell you what I know. Mrs. Carter is doing as well as can be expected. We're unsure how long she was out before calling for help, but she did suffer from mild shock, bruises to her left side and face, and abrasions on both hands."

"But she's doing all right?"

A small frown flickered over the doctor's face. "I suppose all right, considering her condition. I'd like to keep her here for a while longer." She tapped something into the electronic tablet she held, then asked them, "How well do you know Mrs. Carter?"

"I've known her all my life, but we've become good friends in the last five or six years," Savannah replied.

"To be frank, I don't believe I have ever treated any patient her age who has more spunk and determination. I'm astounded the cancer didn't take her a month ago."

"A month ago? She's known about it that long?"

"Well, yes. I diagnosed her with it in late June."

"You did?" Savannah gaped her. "But she only told us about her illness a few days ago."

The doctor studied Savannah's face as she asked, "Has she always been such a strong, determined woman?"

"Yes," Jillian and Savannah answered together.

Dr. Cowan gave them a kind smile, but Jillian thought there was a hint of sadness in it. "I don't pretend to know everything, but I do know the mind plays an important role in our health. Mrs. Carter has survived longer with this illness than most people half her age. But I fear what happened to her last night has weakened her and she's unlikely to rally. In fact, I recommend she go into hospice care when she leaves here. She'll receive good treatment and be far more comfortable there. I can have someone arrange that, if you like."

Savannah fingers tightened around Jillian's, and she sagged against her. "If you think it's for the best," she said faintly.

"Can we see Miss Rita now?" Jillian asked.

The doctor examined the chart again, hesitated a moment, then nodded. "Five minutes. That's it."

"Thank you. Thank you so much." For a moment, Jillian thought Savannah might actually hug the woman.

Inside the hospital room with its drawn curtain and dim light, Miss Rita was a small, frail mound beneath a white sheet, attached to a beeping machine. A clear bag on an IV pole dripped its contents into her veins. Her pale face was bruised and the palms of both hands were heavily bandaged.

Jillian swallowed hard and reached out to grab Savannah's hand. The way Savannah whimpered and clutched her fingers, Jillian knew she felt just as weak and helpless.

"She's asleep," Savannah whispered.

"No, she isn't." Miss Rita's voice was stronger than one might expect. She opened her eyes. Both women gasped and jumped a little. She beckoned with one bandaged hand. "Come closer, girls. Don't make me shout to be heard."

Still holding hands like schoolgirls, they approached her bedside.

"How are you feeling, Miss Rita?" Savannah asked.

She smiled at them. "I'm lying here, idling."

"Is there anything I can get for you?" Jillian asked.

"No, honey. They've got me full of all types of medicine. They come in here every so often to wake me up and ask if I'm having trouble sleeping. Did you ever?" She laughed softly, then stopped and winced. "I have to admit I hurt all over."

"Miss Rita, why on earth were you outside at that time of night?" Jillian asked.

"I heard a noise." She said it as if those simple four words could both answer Jillian's query and set everyone's mind at ease.

"You heard a noise." Savannah studied her face a few seconds. "What kind of noise?"

"In the shed."

Savannah and Jillian exchanged glances.

"You heard something in the shed in the middle of the night?" Jillian asked.

Miss Rita nodded.

"And this sound woke you up?"

"Yes."

"Why, Miss Rita, that shed is a long way from your bedroom. How on earth did you hear a noise from there?"

"Savannah, you know my hearing is keen. It was the middle of the night and dead quiet."

"Do you feel up to telling us what happened, Miss Rita?" Jillian asked. "You know people will want to know."

"I'd rather they have the truth than rumor."

"But don't strain yourself," Savannah said. "You need to rest and—"

Miss Rita wriggled the fingers of one hand as if ridding herself of something annoying. "I'm fine. Just achy and a little tired. So let me talk while I can."

"All right," Savannah said.

"I was already awake, you see. I have trouble sleeping sometimes." She closed her eyes and opened them slowly, as if the lids were heavy. "I heard a thump and a crash in the back, so I got up and looked out the back window. There was a beam from a flashlight moving around inside the shed." She paused and closed her eyes again. "I thought someone was messing with Ryan's car."

"You didn't go out there and confront them, did you?" Jillian asked.

She opened her eyes and fixed her gaze on Jillian. "Why do you think I'm lying in a hospital bed all banged up and bruised?"

"Oh, Miss Rita," Savannah said. "That was a dangerous thing to do. Why did you risk going outside?"

"Because I know everyone in town. Most of them have been my pupils at one time or another. I never thought one of them might hurt me."

"Someone attacked you?" Savannah cried.

"No, no. Nothing like that. I was going to tell them to come back in the daytime if they wanted to see the car."

Savannah let out a long breath and shook her head. "Miss Rita."

"I never got the chance to say a word. Whoever it was must have heard me coming because he rushed out. Startled me so that I toppled over, right smack onto the gravel driveway. I hit the ground hard and my cell phone went flying. Took me a while to get my breath and my wits. Then I had to find the phone."

"You mean you crawled around in the dirt trying to find that phone?"

"I had to, out there in the dark by myself."

"Did you see who it was that was in the shed?"

"No, but I'm sure it was some kid. I noticed some of them gawking in the windows yesterday afternoon."

"Miss Rita, you are amazing." Savannah's eyes were huge as she fixed them on the elderly woman.

"Yes, you are," Jillian said. "But what about the trespasser? Is the sheriff's office trying to find him?"

"Don't be silly. It was a kid, I tell you. I'm sure of it. Tom Shaw is going to go over the car today to see if it's been tampered with . . ." Miss Rita's voice trailed. A tiny frown flickered across her face, and she took in a breath, as if sipping a cool drink. "What did you say?"

"I asked if the sheriff's office is trying to find the intruder."

Something beyond them caught her attention, and she drew in another, deeper breath. "Who's that?"

Jillian glanced over her shoulder and saw no one. "It's just us, Miss Rita," she said turning back to the woman.

Miss Rita seemed not to hear her. "Oh my. Look!" An odd expression passed over her countenance.

"What is it, Miss Rita?" Savannah asked, leaning closer. "Do you need something?"

Miss Rita continued to gaze beyond them. She stretched out one hand.

"You came home." Her voice was barely a whisper, but her face was wreathed in peace, a gentle smile on her lips. "You came home!"

"Miss Rita?"

The beeping of the monitor near the bed slowed, then gave off a high-pitched whine.

Savannah chewed her lip and stared out of the windshield at the hospital. "Whoever was in the shed last night killed Miss Rita."

She and Jillian sat in the hospital parking lot, stunned and grief-stricken by their elderly friend's sudden death. Savannah wept bitterly in the Prius's passenger seat.

"No one killed her," Jillian said softly. Her heart was breaking, but she fought to control her emotions. Savannah needed a strong shoulder.

"But the doctor said all that commotion Miss Rita went through in the middle of the night weakened her to the point she couldn't fight it any longer."

"I know," Jillian said softly, wishing she knew what to say or do. All she could do was let her friend sob, realizing no words could assuage the pain, no gesture would give comfort. After a while, the tears abated and Savannah raised her head. Jillian handed her another fresh tissue.

"We need to let Boone know," Savannah said. She got her phone from her purse and tried calling him again. "Still no answer."

"Maybe he's at work."

"He works nights, remember?" Savannah's eyes filled again.

"Then let's drive by his place."

"Why? Obviously he's not home, Jillian. If he were, he'd answer the phone."

Savannah's snappish words had no effect on Jillian, born as they were from grief. "Let's go see anyway. Maybe he unplugged it or something. In fact, it's possible that he just hasn't heard it ring. He told us last night he has no hearing in one ear. If he's not home, we can leave him a note to get in touch."

"All right, then. Drive past his place."

As they turned down the street where both Miss Rita's and Boone's houses were, Savannah's tears began again. "I don't think I can see her house right now, knowing she'll never be there again."

Jillian was not as close to Miss Rita as Savannah had been, but grief gripped her until she thought she would break. The nearer they drew to Miss Rita's home, the tighter her throat squeezed and the thicker her heartbeat felt. Savannah kept her gaze stubbornly out the other window, but a movement near the house caught Jillian's eye.

"Isn't that Boone on the porch swing?" she said.

"What?" Savannah looked. "It's him. Pull in, please."

Boone watched as Jillian steered into the driveway and stopped.

"Poor Boone," Savannah murmured. She wiped her eyes and nose on a clean tissue. "How am I going to break this to him?"

"I don't know, but we'll do it together."

He stood as they got out of the car. His smile seemed forced, his expression troubled.

"Morning, Jillian. Savannah."

"Good morning, Boone," Jillian said as she and Savannah climbed the porch steps.

"Here." He stepped away from the swing and gestured to it. "Y'all sit here on the porch swing, and I'll grab one of these rockers." He rested one hand on the back of a wooden rocking chair. "Miss Rita isn't up yet, so I'm waiting for her, letting her sleep. She needs that rest."

Savannah met Jillian's eyes, then they settled tensely on the swing.

Boone shifted from one foot to the other. "If y'all would like some sweet tea, I can go over to my house and get some."

"It's okay," Savannah said. "We need to talk to you."

He sat in the old white rocker and fixed his gaze on Savannah. "What's wrong?"

She met his eyes, burst into fresh tears, and buried her face in her hands.

He gaped at Jillian. "Has something happened?" His bright-blue eyes were filled with worry as he glanced back and forth between them. "Is your grandma okay, and Miss Cornelia?"

"They're fine." Jillian swallowed hard. "Boone, we've been trying to call you all morning."

"I take a long walk every morning, weather permitting, and when I got home I did a little yard work while waiting for Miss Rita to wake up. What's going on?"

She cleared her throat. "Did you notice the emergency vehicles last night?"

His eyes got wide. "Here?"

She nodded.

"No. I can't hear out of my left ear, and I sleep soundly. What happened?" His hands curled. "Just tell me what you need to say, Jillian. Don't pretty it up or make it soft. Something happened to Miss Rita, didn't it?"

"Yes. I'm sorry to tell you she passed away earlier this morning in the hospital."

All color drained from his face, and he grew perfectly still. It was as if his heart had stopped pumping, and all his breath had gone. His disbelieving gaze never left her face. "Say what?"

"She's gone," Savannah choked out.

He jumped up and stalked off the porch. He reached the far side of the yard and came back. "She *died*?"

"Yes, Boone," Jillian whispered. "I'm so sorry."

His eyes glittered. "But the doctor said she had a month, maybe more. And she was doing so well you'd never know she was sick."

"I know."

"It makes no sense."

"I know. I'm so sorry."

"Stop saying that!" he shouted. He pivoted sharply and barreled toward his house, disappearing from their view.

"Jillian." Savannah's voice shook. She held out one hand and Jillian gripped it. Her fingers were ice cold. "Do you feel like Miss Rita is going to open that door any minute and offer us some sweet tea?"

Jillian nodded, and they both gazed at the front door with its cheery wreath of silk sunflowers. Miss Rita always changed her wreaths to match the seasons. Jillian sniffled and said nothing. They were silent for a time as the swing rocked them gently back and forth, and the Sunday morning breeze blew warm against their skin. The chains creaked, and birds sang. A car drove by, and church bells rang in the distance. What were they supposed to do now?

"Funny how everything just goes on the same, isn't it?" Savannah asked.

"It is, but that's the way life is."

"Friends and loved ones die every day, leaving a huge gap in the lives of those around them, but for those who didn't know them . . ." Savannah shuddered. "I don't want to think about this."

Jillian squeezed her hand. "Maybe we should go to—"

"Boone's coming back."

The man cut across the yard, head down, hands in the pockets of his jeans. He stopped halfway up the porch stairs. He sat down on the middle step, his back and shoulders rounded. He stared down at his clasped hands as he spoke.

"I reckon having so many people here and all of them eyeballing that car like hungry buzzards did her in. She started to fade. I saw it as soon as everyone began hollerin' about what a mess the car was in, and how beautiful it used to be, and . . . Well, she wanted to go back to the house. She was mighty pale, so I walked her as far as the porch, but then she said she wanted to be alone and sent me back to the shed, told me to keep an eye on things. I bet she was thinking about Ryan again and wondering where he was and if he'd ever come back." He looked up. "I could see she wasn't feeling well. I should've stayed right there with her."

His words cut into Jillian's heart, slicing past her own sorrow, plunging into that helpless place inside her. He had been closer to Miss Rita than anyone, even Savannah. Jillian ached to comfort him.

"Boone, none of this is your fault," Jillian said. "Something happened here in the middle of last night, and that's likely what brought on her sudden decline."

He frowned. "What do you mean? What happened?"

"She heard noises out in the shed, and she went outside to investigate."

"*What?*" He shot to his feet, nearly losing his balance. "Are you telling me she got up out of bed in the middle of the night and came outside to confront someone?"

"That's what she told us," Savannah said. "She said someone came running out and startled her so badly she fell."

Boone clenched and unclenched his hands, pacing and muttering. He faced them, his skin mottled with rage, his eyes blazing. "Did she say who was in that shed?"

Jillian shook her head. "It was dark out. She didn't see."

"Did this person attack her? Hurt her? Why did she come outside? What was she thinking?" He paced as he blurted these questions, the volume of his voice rising with each one.

"No one attacked her," Jillian told him. "She thought it was a kid curious about the car, and he probably heard her footsteps on the gravel driveway. It was pretty cloudy last night, so she couldn't see him."

"Surely he saw her!" Savannah cried. "How could someone

fall down near to someone and that person not hear or see? He should have stopped, seen if she was injured, and taken care of her."

"I agree," Jillian said, "but he was probably scared."

"She fell on that gravel and lay there helpless for a while." Savannah pointed to the driveway. "Then she crawled around to find her phone and call 911."

"Crawled around to find . . ." Boone threw both arms out in a gesture of helpless frustration. "Is that what killed her? She died from that?"

Savannah began to cry again, hard.

He stared at her as if he'd never seen her before, then faced Jillian. "Is it?" he demanded.

Jillian measured her words. "The doctor thinks the experience, coupled with the fall, likely brought on Miss Rita's sudden decline. Plus, as you said, she was already run down from the chaos of yesterday."

At this, Savannah cried even louder. "It's all because of that stupid Buick. If she hadn't given me that car, and if I hadn't insisted on James coming to see it, and if he hadn't told anyone else—"

"Savannah, stop it!" Jillian had never yelled at her friend in her life. But she knew if Savannah continued to give in to this line of thought, she might fall into a dark hole of despair that would be tough to climb out of.

Savannah was so shocked that she froze, gaping at Jillian.

"Miss Rita was old and sick," Jillian said, more calmly. "She gave you the car because she wanted to leave you something that meant a lot to her. She invited some of us here, and word simply got out. Stop blaming yourself for any part of this situation."

Boone stood stock-still, his expression cold and face as gray as marble.

"Don't you be beating yourself up either, Boone. No one is to blame for the way life plays out."

She heard her own words, and she believed them up to a point. But she clung to the thought that if anyone was to blame for Miss Rita's early demise, it was whoever had been in that shed last night. Without him, the woman would have stayed in her bed, slept a good sleep, and awakened feeling stronger. She likely would have lived those extra few weeks.

So, yes. Someone could be blamed. But who?

Boone sank onto the steps again, rested his elbows on his knees and slumped over. Jillian stared at his rounded back. Beside her, Savannah cried silently, staring at nothing.

What was Jillian supposed to say or do that could give either of them any comfort? She didn't even have words to help herself right then. She got up from the swing and went out into the yard. The sun bore down as if to underscore the powerlessness that constricted her thoughts and emotions. Even the sight of Miss Rita's riotous flower beds did nothing to lighten that burden.

She glanced toward the shed. Something about it was off. For a moment, she was confused. Then she realized the double doors stood ajar. Never in her memory had Miss Rita left the doors standing open when no one was around, not even a few inches. She must have forgotten to lock them. Or perhaps someone had fiddled with the lock and broken in. Either way, they'd woken poor Miss Rita from her sleep.

Jillian approached the shed with concern and trepidation. Someone had been in that old building in the middle hours of the previous night. Who had it been, and why had they gone inside? The car was there, of course, but it wasn't running. Had the intruder tried to steal parts from the engine? Maybe word had spread about the lockbox and he had prowled inside, searching for more hidden treasures.

She paused at the door, noting the lock and chain that dangled from the clasp that held them. Her inexperienced eye spotted no marks to indicate the lock had been picked. How had the intruder even gotten in?

Another unwelcome and troublesome thought leaped into her mind. Was it possible an intruder was in there now, watching the trio on the porch, waiting for them to leave so he could prowl and pilfer?

The notion was so unlikely she was almost able to dismiss it. She swallowed hard and reached to open one door.

"Don't touch it!"

She shrieked and jumped back, bumping into Boone's large body. "Geez, Boone, you scared the daylights out of me."

He nodded toward the shed. "Let's make sure there is nothing or no one in there to hurt you."

So she hadn't been the only one entertaining such worrisome ideas. He pulled open both doors and daylight fell on the dusty contents, but no intruder lurked in the shadows.

"Someone was going through all this junk last night," Jillian said. "That's what all the noise was that Miss Rita heard. And they just threw everything around willy-nilly. What a mess."

"I'll clean it up, Jillian. Don't worry." He went inside and walked around, eyeing the disarray. He turned to the car, lifted the hood and scanned the engine. "I don't think whoever it was hurt anything."

"Oh, but look," Jillian said, peering in the back window. "The seats have been ripped even more."

"Likely hoping for more treasure," Savannah said as she joined them. "Whoever it was got the front seats *and* the back."

Jillian groaned as she peeked in through the window. "I wonder if they found anything."

"Miss Rita might have scared them off before they did," Boone said, scowling at the car.

Savannah gulped in a shaky breath.

Jillian touched her shoulder. "You okay?"

"No, but I will be. Boone, did I hear you say you'd clean this up?"

He nodded. "I'll do it today." He glanced around. "But I doubt whoever did this will be back. It's pretty obvious nothing of value is here, except for the Riviera."

"The shed was open," Jillian said.

"It was? Miss Rita won't like that." Savannah broke off suddenly and bit her lower lip. "I mean . . ."

"It didn't get locked up after everyone left yesterday, I guess." Boone seemed uneasy. "I'll make sure it's locked from here on out." No one spoke for a bit. Emotions lay raw across his face. "I need to go home now," he choked out.

They walked out of the shed, and without another word, he closed the doors, locked the chain, and hurried away.

"Poor Boone," Savannah said.

Poor Moss Hollow. There would never be another Miss Rita.

That afternoon at Belle Haven, Jillian and Savannah once again examined the contents of the lockbox that had been found in the car.

"You said the sheriff had you e-mail him photos of the contents of this box?" Savannah asked.

"I suppose that means he's going to try to find out if that stuff was stolen."

"But even he if finds that it was, he can't arrest anyone."

"True, but he can return the items to their owners."

They were on the sofa in the sitting room, the box resting on the cushion between them. Bertie was nearby, thumbing through a cookbook for what she called "a new spin on leftover pinto beans." Cornelia sat in a chair, tatting edging for a white blouse she thought was too plain. Possum was stretched out on the arm of the chair, his blue eyes watching thread fly through the shuttle, his tail twitching as if he were waiting for the right moment to pounce.

"What else could it be but stolen?" Cornelia asked. "Money and jewelry tucked away out of sight like that, in a place no one would ever think to look for it."

"Maybe the owner was afraid it would be stolen and stashed it." Jillian wrinkled her nose. "That sounds lame, doesn't it? Do you think someone would actually sneak into a car, hack open the upholstery, cut out springs, and hide a box full of valuables? Wouldn't digging a hole in the backyard and burying it make more sense?"

Cornelia peered at her, her expression full of speculation. "I'm not so curious about why the things were hidden as much as I'd like to know who hid them."

"Good point," Bertie said. "I'd think it would take a wacky person to do that if those things weren't stolen."

"And leave the box there all these years," Cornelia added. "What happened to whoever it was that hid that stuff? Why didn't they come back for it?"

"Maybe the sheriff will find out something," Bertie said as she continued to leaf through the cookbook.

"I hope so." Cornelia wiggled her shoulders, but her shuttle never faltered. "Sometimes, curiosity makes me itch something fierce."

"Take an oatmeal bath," Bertie suggested. "Best thing for itchy curiosity."

Jillian realized the twins were trying to lighten the atmosphere a little and lift everyone's spirits. She and Savannah exchanged a smile.

"Bless their hearts," Savannah whispered. She ran her fingers over the box and blew out a deep breath. "We need to look at these things, but I sure don't want to."

"Do it anyway," Cornelia said.

"I feel like I'm—oh, I don't know exactly—it's like handling something that doesn't belong to me or going through someone's medicine cabinet. It doesn't feel right."

Bertie held her finger on the page she was perusing and glanced up. "It's yours now, honey. Wherever that money came from, and whoever that jewelry belonged to—why, if Coy thought it belonged to someone after all this time, he would have taken it with him. I bet he's only doing a cursory investigation to put your mind at rest."

"That's true," Jillian said. "If the owner hid it, they must not have valued it very much. And if it was stolen, the thief is doubtless long gone from our neck of the woods."

Savannah wrinkled her nose as if the contents had a particular stink to them. "I know, but still." Nevertheless, she opened the box and poked around with one finger.

Jillian picked up a stack of bills. They were old, wrinkled, and soft. The latest print date she found on any of them was 1972. She set them on the coffee table and sat back.

"Raymond says spend the money and wear the jewelry," Cornelia said. She glanced at Savannah as she stroked Possum's cream-colored fur. "Trust him."

Savannah gave her a smile and said, "Tell Raymond thank you for his concern."

"Hear that?" Cornelia said to Possum. That cat stretched out on the arm of the chair and closed his eyes. Jillian could hear him purring from where she sat.

"You'd better take that to the bank as soon as it opens tomorrow," Bertie said to Savannah. "You can't just have money and jewelry lying around that way. Someone with bad intentions and no character will hear about it and come after it."

"I've been thinking about what to do with it." Savannah picked up the smaller of the two necklaces and watched the sapphire catch the light. "I might wear this one. It's pretty. But this big one, though . . ." She held it up and dangled it from her index finger. "It might be worth a lot of money, but it's gaudier than all get-out, don't you think?"

Bertie tipped her head to one side, considering it. "I'd never wear it. Not styled like that. But you could get those stones reset into several different pieces."

"That's what I was thinking," Jillian said.

"Great minds do think alike, honey." Bertie smiled.

Savannah laid the necklaces side by side on the coffee table, adding the string of pearls beside the other two pieces. She stretched out their chains to the full length, then fingered the bills, her face thoughtful. "Money never goes out of style."

"That's the honest truth," Cornelia said. "Unless it's Confederate money, and I bet even then it might be worth something to a collector."

"These are old, used bills, but they are definitely worth their face value." Savannah stared at the cash for a while. "You know what? This would make a nice donation to Miss Rita's church."

"Yes, it would," Bertie said approvingly.

"I think that is a lovely idea." Cornelia laid down her tatting and beamed at Savannah. "That congregation is so small, and they don't have a lot of money for updates or repairs."

"Exactly. Miss Rita told me when it rains, everyone has to sit on one side of the sanctuary because the roof leaks so badly on the other side. And the appliances in the church kitchen are so old I'm surprised they still work."

Jillian gazed at the metal box and chewed her lower lip. Donating it to Miss Rita's church was a wonderful idea, but still, Savannah could use that money too. Restoring the Riviera would be a fairly expensive undertaking. And there was her upcoming wedding to James, which was a costly event no matter how unfussy their plans were. "Are you sure you want to give this away?" Jillian asked, feeling compelled to play devil's advocate. "You could use some of it to—"

"Yes. I'm sure." Savannah responded so quickly, so forcefully that she must have been having the same conversation internally. "I've been getting along just fine up to this point, and I will continue to get along just fine. I'm giving it—all of it—to the Rock Valley Methodist Church in honor of Miss Rita."

Without another word, Savannah gathered the contents of the lockbox, replaced them, and closed the lid.

Miss Rita's memorial service was held the following Tuesday in the high school auditorium—the only venue in town large enough to accommodate the scores of mourners.

Rather than a service full of gloom and despair and talk of death, Miss Rita's funeral overflowed with stories and remembrances of her life. By the time it was over, aching hearts had been warmed with a cache of fond memories and the united spirit of those who loved her. Boone was the only mourner who kept to himself, and he went home as soon as the graveside service was over.

"I worry about that boy," Cornelia said that evening in Belle Haven's sitting room. Several Southern Sweetie Pies and other friends had gathered there. "I wish he had come here this evening instead of staying all by himself. He's never had many people in his life, and now it's like he's lost his mama twice."

"I invited him for supper," Bertie said, "but he said he needed to be by himself."

"Poor fella." Savannah sighed. "But we all handle our grief in different ways, and everyone should try to understand that. For myself, I appreciate having my loved ones around me."

"This hasn't been easy on you either," Bertie said. "We're glad you're here with us."

"Amen to that," Lenora said. "We lean on one another, and it gives us such blessed comfort."

Others nodded, murmuring agreement.

"Can I get anyone another piece of cake? Some coffee?" Lenora had spent most of that day waiting on her friends. Jillian stood and rested both hands on her shoulders and guided her to the nearest chair.

"You sit there," she said. "I'll bring *you* some coffee and cake for once."

"Oh, but—"

"No arguments. Sit."

When Jillian returned with Lenora's refreshments and sat down, Maudie asked, "Does anyone know if Larry Don Benning is an heir or something?"

"He's probably an 'heir or something' to someone in his family, but I doubt he's one of Miss Rita's heirs," Savannah said.

"Well, he must think he is," Wanda Jean said, passing a significant look to the group over the rim of her coffee cup.

Annalise frowned in confusion. "Why would you say that?"

Wanda Jean and Maudie exchanged glances as if debating whether or not to share the news. Jillian bit her lip to keep from saying anything while they waited.

"After the graveside service," Maudie said, "we overheard him asking Miss Rita's minister about the reading of the will."

"Are you kidding?" Savannah sounded outraged.

"You heard him ask who, what, where?" Jillian asked, similarly shocked.

Lenora's face was thunderous. "What business is it of Mr.

Larry Don Benning?" She turned to Bertie. "If that man shows up at my funeral, you kick him right on out the door."

"We'll cross that bridge when we get to it. What did Pastor Julie tell him, Wanda Jean?"

"I tried to hear, but she led Larry Don away from the rest of us. When I got closer, she pulled him away even farther."

"Well, I don't blame her," Lenora said. "A graveside is not the place to be asking about wills and sticking noses into other people's businesses."

"We weren't sticking our noses into other people's business," Maudie said. "We were trying to find out facts." She leaned toward Savannah. "I'll bet you're in the will, aren't you?"

Savannah shifted in her chair. "I really do not want to talk about this. If we can't remember Miss Rita for the life she lived, then I think we should just all go home." She got up and practically ran out of the room.

Jillian hurried out after her. Savannah rushed up the stairs and into Jillian's bedroom, with Jillian on her heels.

"Shut the door," Savannah said. "Keep them out of here, please."

Jillian closed the door quietly and sank down on the bed beside her distraught friend. Savannah's eyes were dry but her face was scarlet, her hands clenched tightly in her lap.

"What is *wrong* with some people?" Savannah asked. "Do they have to act like a bunch of vultures? Miss Rita wasn't wealthy with piles of money in the bank. And why does anyone care what someone else might inherit?"

Jillian rubbed Savannah's tense back. "I know. Sometimes, these types of situations bring out the worst in people."

"Cold, hard greed disguised as simple 'interest.'" Savannah shook her head.

"In Maudie and Wanda Jean's case, they do care about others. It's not greed. They're just . . ."

"Nosy."

"I was going to say curious."

"Nosy says it better. Larry Don is neither nosy nor caring. He's just plain greedy."

"I know."

They sat in silence for a couple minutes.

"I could tell those nosy—er, *curious* women what they want to know," Savannah said.

Jillian raised her eyebrows.

"The reading of the will is tomorrow morning at ten o'clock."

Jillian nodded. "Gary Moody called me late this afternoon. I didn't expect to receive a bequest."

"He called every beneficiary today." Savannah met Jillian's eyes. "I'm not saying a word to anyone else about it, though. I mean, really. If they knew, the whole town would show up with their hands out. They probably will anyway."

Savannah was rarely so caustic, but Jillian fully understood her mood. Her friend's face was no longer red but pale and drawn, emphasizing the dark smudges beneath her eyes. Her usual warm smile was nowhere to be seen. Considering her lack of sleep, an abundance of stress, worry about Miss Rita, and then witnessing the woman's sudden death, it was no wonder Savannah was so pallid and her words so bitter.

"You'll be there, right?" Savannah asked. "Because without you, I might just say words I can never take back."

Jillian put an arm around her friend's shoulder and squeezed. "Of course I'll be there."

Gary Moody was a tall, lanky redheaded lawyer in his late thirties. Dressed in a light-blue seersucker suit, he leaned against the corner of his desk and watched as the beneficiaries filed into his office and sat down. Every one of them eyed him with varying degrees of expectancy.

He glanced over their heads and spoke to the young woman standing just inside the open doorway. "I believe everyone is here, Marcia."

"Yes, sir." She gave everyone a brief, professional smile and backed out of the room, closing the door behind her.

Savannah leaned close to Jillian's ear and whispered, "There aren't as many as I expected." She glanced around. "And no one seems particularly happy to be here."

"Of course not. We'd all rather have Miss Rita with us."

Savannah played with the sapphire pendant that hung from her neck. She had polished the silver chain until it gleamed like new. She had told Jillian earlier that morning she was wearing it because something about it gave her a feeling of peace.

On Jillian's other side, Cornelia fiddled nervously with her purse strap. Bertie and Lenora had been notified they were receiving bequests, but had stayed at The Chocolate Shoppe. Gary would deliver to them whatever Miss Rita's will dictated. Cornelia had expressed several times that morning that receiving an inheritance from Miss Rita made her uneasy. When pressed for reasons, she shook her head. "I don't know why. I just don't feel like she's gone."

Jillian had no satisfactory reply for that and reminded herself Cornelia's thoughts often strayed in a netherworld that only she understood.

The attorney glanced over everyone present, then moved behind his desk. He thumbed through a document, then passed another gaze over them as he sat down. His smile was sad and brief.

"Our community has lost one of its most beloved members.

Miss Rita Carter will be sorely missed." There was a long pause in which several tissues and handkerchiefs came out of pockets, including Gary's. He cleared his throat and began reading.

Miss Rita had thoughtfully divided her belongings, including monetary bequests to her church and the local animal shelter. She left Bertie and Cornelia her extensive recipe collection and some unique bakeware. To Lenora, she bequeathed a collection of Depression-era glassware.

Gary continued reading aloud. "'For Jillian Green, whose red hair, bright smile, and funny antics kept me entertained so often over the years, I leave my collection of *Little House* books. You will never need to borrow anyone's copies again.'"

"My goodness." Tears stung Jillian's eyes. "That's the sweetest thing."

"'For Savannah Cantrell, daughter of my heart, I leave the contents of safe-deposit box number 674 in the Moss Hollow Savings & Loan.'"

Savannah clutched Jillian's hand.

"'All contents inside my house, with the exclusion of the above mentioned bequests, go to my dearest friend, Boone Hackett, to keep, sell, barter, or otherwise handle as he chooses.'"

Boone dropped his head and stared at the floor, his face and ears red.

"'Lastly, I leave my home and remaining property at 305 Willow Avenue to Allison Vinton.'"

Forehead creased in confusion, Jillian said what she figured everybody else was wondering too. "Who in the world is Allison Vinton?"

With the exception of the lawyer, everyone in the room glanced around as if expecting the unknown person to stand up and introduce herself.

"Ms. Vinton is unwilling to come forward at this time and prefers this business to be dealt with via phone calls, online correspondence, and the United States Postal System," Gary said.

"But who is she?" Jillian asked. "I've never heard of her."

"Neither have I." Boone's frown was deep.

"Me neither," Savannah said. In fact, from the murmurs sweeping the room, no one had heard of her.

"She's someone Miss Rita has known for a long time," Gary said, "and she wanted to provide something for her."

"But—" Savannah started.

Gary put up a hand. "I'm sorry, but I've agreed to confidentiality regarding Ms. Vinton's whereabouts and connection to Miss Rita. Unless and until Ms. Vinton agrees that the information is no longer to be kept confidential, I can say no more about her. Now, do any of you have other questions or concerns?" No one spoke. "Very well. Most of you may pick up your bequests here. Savannah, I'll need to go with you to the bank for you to retrieve the contents of the safe-deposit box. See Marcia about an appointment to do that. Boone, as soon as you have emptied the house and shed, please turn over any and all keys to the property to me." The attorney paused and lifted one brow. "I trust this will be done in an expedient manner so there'll be no trouble? I'll see to it that Ms. Vinton gets the keys."

Boone nodded woodenly and then left the room without saying a word to anyone.

"I imagine he thought he'd be getting that house," an elderly member of Rock Valley Methodist Church said.

"Did you see his face?" Jillian whispered to Savannah.

She nodded. "I assumed Miss Rita would leave the house to him."

"I imagine everyone else thought the same."

"But he didn't seem angry."

"No, just hurt."

Jillian, Cornelia, and Savannah were the last ones to leave Gary's office, and they lingered while he said goodbye to the others.

"Gary," Savannah said, "we've known each other for a long time."

"Yes, we have, and I'm aware how close you were to Miss Rita in these last years. I'm sorry for your loss."

"Thank you. The town will miss her."

"Indeed. My father said she was one of his favorite teachers." He smiled. "She had retired by the time I would have been in her class, sorry to say. She has been my client since I set up practice, and I've never known a finer woman."

Savannah chewed her lower lip as if contemplating her next words. "I don't know if you realize this, but I've done Miss Rita's taxes and helped her with her bookkeeping for several years."

"I was aware of that, yes."

"We used to talk a lot, and she became a dear friend. She never shared much about her life with many people, but she told me a lot of things she never told anyone else. In all this time, I've never heard her mention someone named Allison Vinton."

"I understand."

Understand? Jillian frowned. *Understand what?*

"Do you know this Vinton woman?" Cornelia piped up.

Gary shot her a quick glance. "I've spoken with her on the phone a few times. We've yet to meet face-to-face."

"Does she live nearby?" Savannah asked.

"I can't say."

"Can't say, or won't say?"

"In this case, Savannah, it amounts to the same thing." He gave her a quizzical expression. "Does it bother you that Miss Rita did not leave her house and property to you?"

Savannah's cheeks flamed, and she stiffened. "Of course not."

"Why, forevermore. You've got some nerve accusing our Savannah of something so mean." Cornelia's blue eyes blazed as she glared at him.

He gave her a mild smile.

"I never even considered that she might leave it to me," Savannah said. "I figured it would go to Boone. She was far closer to him than to anyone else, even me."

"That's true." Gary's even voice continued to reveal nothing.

"What bothers me is that Miss Rita was always a logical, thoughtful person," she continued. "She had a good hold on her wits, and I never saw a sign of any weakening of her mind. So I fail to understand why she would leave her house to a stranger. It makes no sense."

"I can see why you'd think that," the attorney said.

"But it makes sense to you?"

Again, he merely smiled.

Jillian nudged Savannah gently. "I think we should leave," she murmured.

"I think we should get to the bottom of this," Cornelia said. "And this stranger, whoever she is, is at the bottom of it, I can promise you that."

"Now, Miss Cornelia, there's no reason for you to get yourself worked up."

She narrowed her eyes at the lawyer. "Don't you talk to me like that, Gary Moody. I'll get worked up if I want to."

He blinked. "No offense, ma'am. I'm just saying that the situation is under control, and you needn't be concerned."

"Would you please ask this Vinton woman to e-mail or call me?" Savannah said before Cornelia spoke again. She pulled out a business card from her purse and handed it to Gary.

"I'll give her your message. Sorry, I can't do any more than that."

"See that you do." Cornelia stalked away, nose in the air. "Uppity young man."

In the car, Jillian and Savannah got out their cell phones while Cornelia fumed in the back seat, muttering about Raymond and Possum. Jillian hoped she'd calm down. Cornelia could be a force to be reckoned with when she got her dander up, and Jillian didn't want to participate in that reckoning.

"Some people forget we can find out nearly anything online," Savannah said as she and Jillian each began their own online searches.

A few moments later, the name Allison Vinton produced results on both screens. "Here's a schoolteacher in Washington." Jillian tapped the link, and read the small bit of information available. "It says nothing other than she teaches middle school."

"This one is a registered nurse in England. I hardly think Miss Rita would leave her house to someone over there."

"Here's another. She's a real-estate developer in—"

"Can you believe him?" Savannah asked suddenly. "He is actually watching us. What does he think we are, spies?"

Jillian looked up at Savannah's sharp tone and saw Gary Moody standing near the large plate glass window of his reception room. He sipped coffee, but his unsmiling gaze was focused on them. "He knows what we're doing," she said.

"I'm sure. If he'd just answered my questions, we wouldn't have to waste time trying to find out who she is. And where she is."

Cornelia rapped on her window as if that would send him on his way. "Does he think we're going to kidnap that woman if we find out who she is?"

"I'm sure he doesn't think that," Jillian said. "Don't get too upset. He has rules he has to observe just like anyone else, and he's not going to violate them. He could get his license revoked if he did."

"I know." Savannah sighed and put her phone aside. "It's up to us to find out what we need to know, but I don't want to do it here. He's liable to come out and demand we turn off our phones."

"I'll take a swing at him with my pocketbook," Cornelia declared. "It's heavy enough to make him back off. I put an orange in there in case I got hungry before we went home. One of those big oranges, like a softball."

This produced a laugh between them, easing the moment.

"I feel a need for a bear claw and a large coffee," Jillian said.

"Sounds heavenly," Savannah agreed.

"How about you, Aunt Cornelia? Are you going to eat your orange or would you rather have a doughnut?"

"No, thank you. Take me home, please," Cornelia said. "I need Raymond."

Jillian drove to Belle Haven and dropped off Cornelia, and then she and Savannah went to the bakery. They had to park a block away from The Chocolate Shoppe, and when they stepped inside, they found every table full. It was standing room only.

"This place is jumping," Jillian said. "I'd better go see if my help is needed in the kitchen." She glanced toward the corner. "There are a couple of empty chairs at Stewie's table. He's so engrossed in the newspaper I doubt he'd mind if you sat there. I'll join you, if I get a free minute."

Savannah nodded and crossed the room to where the old man sat. Jillian hurried back to the kitchen. The heat greeted her like a steamy fist, and the yeasty fragrance of fresh bread reminded her she'd skipped breakfast that morning. She reached for an apron.

Bertie was taking a large pan of dinner rolls from the oven.

"How'd it go? And while you tell me about it, go ahead and frost those loaves, will you?" She dipped her head toward several loaves of raisin bread on a cooling rack. "You'll have to make the icing because I used the last of it earlier on the cinnamon rolls. Lenora is on a delivery to Pat Hinkle's house, so I'm glad you're here. That raisin bread is a special order and being picked up soon." She glanced at the clock. "Goodness! They'll be here in about fifteen minutes."

"I'll hurry." While Jillian whipped up the icing, she told Bertie what had happened in Gary Moody's office. When she got to the part about Allison Vinton, Bertie stopped working and gawked at her.

"Do you mean to stand there on your two feet and tell me that house went to a perfect stranger and not Boone Hackett?"

"That's what I mean to tell you." Jillian began to drizzle precise lines of white icing onto the tops of the raisin bread loaves. "We found three Allison Vintons online, but didn't get much information about any of them."

"Forevermore." Bertie stood, resting her fists on either hip, her face a mask of bewilderment. "How'd Boone take it?"

"He left right away. Didn't say anything."

"He wouldn't, of course. I'd have thought if Miss Rita didn't leave the place to Boone, she'd have left it to Savannah."

"I thought so too, and so did everyone who was there."

"What about Savannah? Was she upset?"

"Confused is more like it. Not because she didn't get the house, but because she has no idea who this person is or why she inherited Miss Rita's home."

Bertie heaved out a hard breath, a frown deepening between her brows. "What did you say this person's name is?"

"Allison Vinton." She glanced up. "Have you ever heard of her?"

Bertie frowned in thought for a while, then finally shook her head. "No. I don't know anyone with the name of Vinton. What did Gary say about her?"

"Gary wouldn't tell us a thing."

"Well, why ever not?" Bertie went back to laying the rolls out on a cooling rack. "He's always been a such good, polite boy."

"It's not that, Bertie. There's a confidentiality agreement he can't breach."

"What a lot of hooey."

"Maybe so, but it's the law."

"Sometimes, the law is . . ."

"Unfair?"

"I was going to say foolish, but unfair is accurate too. Not all the time, granted, like when a crime has been committed, but in cases like this—well, I think there's room for improvement."

"But when you think about it, Bertie, even if it seems foolish, or unfair, or even maddening, it's really no one else's business what Miss Rita chose to do with her own property. And if the person she gave it to doesn't want to come forward publicly, then she shouldn't have to just to satisfy our curiosity. No law has been broken, and I figure she's got a good reason for wanting to stay behind the scenes."

Bertie gave her sharp look. "Why do you pick right now to show off your good sense?"

Jillian laughed. "Because my grandmother taught me how to think."

"So, are you going to try to get in touch with any of these Allison Vintons you found online?"

"No ma'am. It might not be against the law for me to do so, but if she doesn't want to be reached, then I won't try."

Jillian was piping the last row of icing when Savannah burst into the kitchen.

"Come out here, Jillian. Stewie Franks knows something you've just got to hear."

13

Savannah's face was flushed, her eyes wide. She practically vibrated where she stood. Jillian couldn't tell if her excitement was from agitation or eagerness.

"Can it wait? Bertie needs me to—"

"No, no, honey. Go with Savannah." Bertie made a shooing gesture with both hands. "This sounds important. Besides, you got those loaves frosted, and I've got the dinner rolls ready. I'm about caught up, and Lenora should be back soon. Go."

Savannah grabbed her hand and pulled her along so enthusiastically Jillian nearly tripped over her own feet.

"Mornin'," Stewie greeted when they reached his table. "It's not often I get to have two pretty ladies sitting with me."

"What is it with you fellas in Moss Hollow?" Jillian grinned at him. "Just a bunch of flirts."

He chuckled, his faded eyes twinkling. "I put in my hearing aids for you two. I don't do that for just anyone."

"We thank you kindly." Savannah patted his left hand. "Now, would you please tell Jillian what you just told me?"

"All of it?"

"Yes, please. If you don't mind."

"I don't mind. But first, I'd like a refill on this coffee."

"How about a bear claw too?" Jillian offered. "On the house. I'll get it."

His eyes lit up and she went to get coffee and pastries for all three of them.

"Okay, Stewie. What is it Savannah wants you to tell me?" Jillian asked when she returned. She bit gratefully into her bear claw. It was nearly noon—she should have waited and bought a tuna sandwich at the deli. She should have had breakfast. She should drink milk instead of more coffee.

I should stop telling myself what I should've done.

"I was admiring that necklace Savannah's wearing. It's right pretty, don't you think?"

Jillian nodded. "Yes, it sure is."

Stewie stirred in sugar and tasted his coffee. He added another packet and stirred slowly, deliberately, as if the beverage was the only thing on his mind. Savannah and Jillian traded glances. Both knew Stewie was not someone who could be rushed, in either word or deed.

"Yes, indeed, that necklace caught my interest the minute she sat down here." He sipped his coffee. "You wanna know why?"

"I sure do."

"Well, I'll tell you." He took a big bite out of the bear claw and studied the pastry from every angle as he chewed. "No doubt about it—y'all make the best one of these I ever ate, and that's a fact."

Savannah fidgeted, but Jillian gave him a smile. "Thanks, Stewie. We try to make everything the best."

"Well, sure you do." He laid down the bear claw and wiped his fingers on a napkin. "Anyways, that necklace caught my attention for more reasons than one."

Jillian cupped her chin in her hand and raised both eyebrows. "And what reasons are those?"

"Well, I'll tell you."

"I wish you would," Savannah murmured.

He grinned and tapped the end of her nose as if she were a toddler. "Ah, I'm just playing with you, girl. Trying to bring a smile to your sad face. I know these last few days have been hard on you. Anyway, Jillian, I recognize that necklace."

Jillian sat straight up. "You do?"

"Yup. I ought to recognize it. I bought it for my wife for our tenth wedding anniversary."

Jillian felt her eyes widen. "You did?"

He nodded. "Had it made especially for her. Her birthday was in September, so sapphire was her birthstone. I was born in April, so mine is a diamond. She was the center of my life and I wanted to always be around her, so I came up with the idea of a sapphire in the middle and teeny diamonds around it."

"Stewie, that is one of the sweetest things I've ever heard." Savannah sniffed as she raised her arms to open the clasp.

"What're you doing?"

"I'm giving it back to you."

He caught her left arm. "No you're not, so don't take it off."

"But you—"

"I'm sure not going to wear it, if that's what you're thinking. It wouldn't go with a scrap of clothing I have."

"Oh, Stewie." Savannah laughed softly. "But it was your wife's, and it's so special to you."

"And now I want it to be special to you. Let's pretend you gave it back to me, and I took it and wrapped it up in a package all pretty with a bow and everything, and handed it to you. Now it's a special present so you can remember me after I'm gone."

"Stewie." She blinked hard.

"Keep it. Please."

Savannah dropped her hands to the table, tears swimming in her brown eyes. "Thank you. I will cherish it so very much." She swallowed hard and blotted a napkin against her cheeks. "I have never wept as much in my life as I have this last week." She sniffled. "But, Stewie, please finish telling Jillian the rest."

Jillian nodded with enthusiasm. "Please do."

"Well, young lady, I will. We were robbed." He took another

bite of the bear claw and consumed it leisurely, washing it down with another couple sips of coffee.

Jillian waited him out. Savannah played with the pendant, her eyes on their elderly companion. One leg jiggled beneath the table, but other than that, she sat still.

"No, that's not exactly right, is it? We were burgled. If you're home, you're robbed. If you're gone, you're burgled."

Jillian nodded.

"We weren't home, I believe, because we don't know when it happened," he continued. "One night we were getting dressed up to go out for supper, and Jenny said to me, 'Honey, where'd you put my necklace?'" He leaned forward and met Jillian's eyes. "I hadn't put it anywhere." He sat back and waited for her response.

"You hadn't?"

"Nope. We searched high and low for it, then Jenny said, 'Honey, Grandma's Jezebel is missing too.'"

"Grandma's Jezebel?" Jillian asked.

"Yeah, it was an ugly old necklace that belonged to Jenny's great-grandma." He put down his coffee cup and measured with his hands. "It was this big, with lots of glass stones and brass curlicues and whatnot. It was so gaudy and glittery that no one wanted to wear the thing. Jenny's family called it Grandma's Jezebel. Losing it didn't bother me one bit. It was ugly as sin and nearly worthless."

What about the money? The pearls? Jillian thought.

As if reading her mind, he said "And then Jenny got all big-eyed and white-faced, like she'd seen ghost, and she tore into the dresser drawers. In two minutes, she had all our socks and pajamas and such in a pile on the floor. Then she sat down right flat on the floor next to it and bawled her eyes out." He glanced at his nearly empty cup. "Think I could have a refill?"

Tamping down her impatience, Jillian got up and filled his cup. He went through the same ritual of adding sugar and tasting until he was satisfied.

"You said Jenny was bawling her eyes out," Jillian prompted.

"Yep. Broke my heart seeing her that way. That little old necklace was kinda pricey for our budget, but I promised I'd have another made. Losing that Jezebel was no great loss, let me tell you. But that's not what broke her heart."

"No?"

"Nope." Stewie took a sip of coffee. "See, unbeknownst to me, Jenny had been putting aside money for years. Spare change and dollars here and there. When she'd have twenty or thirty bucks, she'd take it to the bank or the store and trade it for bigger bills, then she'd hide that money in her dresser drawer."

"And you didn't know she had it?"

"Not the least idea. But she was so broken up, I didn't even scold her for keeping it in the dresser instead of in the bank. It wasn't the wisest thing for her to do, but I'm sure she had her reasons. She felt so bad, I couldn't make her feel worse by hollering about it."

"Of course not," Savannah murmured.

"But why?" Jillian asked. "I mean why was she saving it?"

"She had started saving the first month we got married. Her idea was that one day she'd surprise me with the money, and we'd use it for something important. Pay off the house, or go on a cruise, or maybe buy a car."

"That was quite a pile of money to have saved up back then," Savanah said.

"I know it. She was a homemaker and she was thrifty, plus she did little odd jobs for people on the side. Baking a cake or cleaning someone's house or making a dress, that kind of thing. After she'd take out the tithe for the church offering from whatever she earned, she'd spend a little and save the rest of it. That, along with any spare change she got from grocery shopping and whatnot."

"And you didn't know she was doing it?" Jillian asked.

"Nope. I knew about the odd jobs, of course, but I thought she was buying shoes or books or doodads for the house or something."

"So you reported this theft to the sheriff, didn't you?"

"Yeah, but that was back when Pointer was sheriff, and he wasn't really what you might call a straight shooter. Nothing got done about that thievery. I doubt they even tried to find out who took our stuff."

Jillian frowned. "But surely there was a report on file."

Stewie shrugged. "Don't matter now. I miss Jenny something fierce, and I wish we'd been able to have children, but other than that, I like my life as it is—simple and easy. I've got my routine, I've got my friends. It's enough."

"Bless your heart, Stewie." Savannah gave him a smile that trembled. "I'm glad you've found contentment." Her voice cracked and she stood. "Excuse me. I need to go comb my hair or something."

"Poor girl," he said as they watched her hurry toward the restroom. "She's taking Miss Rita's death mighty hard, isn't she?"

"She is." Jillian's heart ached a little.

Stewie ate the last of his bear claw, drained his coffee, and wiped his fingers on a napkin. Jillian knew it was time to get back to work, but she could tell he had more to say. "Stewie, do you have even an inkling of who might have taken your things?" she asked.

"Nope. I didn't back then, and I still don't. Like I said, it doesn't matter."

Something about the way he shifted in his chair and refused to meet her eyes underscored Jillian's fresh suspicions. He wasn't telling her everything he knew, and she wondered how to worm it out of him. Or if she even could. Stewie Franks was far more than the kindly old man he appeared to be. He was clever and thoughtful, and very little managed to get past his sharp observation.

Jillian cleared her throat. "One more question."

"What's that?" He pulled out a pocket watch and squinted at the face for a few seconds before tucking it back in. "I need to get home and check on Tiger. Darn cat gets anxious if I'm gone very long."

"Do you know anyone by the name of Allison Vinton?"

He blinked as if she'd blown a puff of air in his eyes, then shook his head. "Nope."

"You're sure?"

"Yep. Why?"

"Miss Rita willed her house to someone named Allison Vinton."

He stared at her. "Say what?"

She repeated the words. "Do you know why she'd do that?"

"I assume she had her reasons."

"Stewie."

"Jillian."

"You know something."

"I know lots of things. But that doesn't mean I'm telling them." He stood up. "Thank you kindly for the bear claw and the coffee."

Savannah came rushing back to the table. "Wait a minute, Stewie."

"I gotta get back to Tiger." He started to move away.

"Just one thing." She pulled her checkbook out of her purse, quickly wrote a check and held it out to him. "This is the amount that was found in that lockbox, and it belongs to you."

He took a step back and shook his head. "Nope. I don't want it."

"Please. It's money that Jenny scrimped and saved for years."

"I don't want it. I don't need it. You keep it. Go buy yourself a new wardrobe or television or computer or something."

"But Stewie, I can't keep this money. It doesn't belong to me."

He gave her a shrewd look. "What were you going to do with it before you found out where it came from? Hide it under a mattress?"

"I was going to make a donation to the Rock Valley Methodist Church in memory of Miss Rita."

"Good. You do that. Those pearls, though. They're the real deal. Jenny's daddy gave them to her on our wedding day. If you don't want to wear them, then sell them and give that money to the church too." He glanced back and forth between them, then gave a single sharp nod. "I don't want to talk about any of this anymore. You hear me?" And with that, he left The Chocolate Shoppe.

14

Savannah rang the doorbell soon after the supper hour that evening. Jillian noticed that her friend seemed tired and distracted as they went to join the others in the sitting room.

"We were going to watch *All About Eve*," Cornelia said as soon as she saw Savannah. "Come in and watch it with us. Lenora's here too. We had a light supper so we can have lots of popcorn and cookies tonight."

"Sounds like fun," Savannah said with forced brightness in her voice. "James has come down with a stomach virus, so he's staying away from me for a while."

"Well, bless his heart." Cornelia got up. "Have a seat, honey, and I'll go get you some lemonade. Or would you rather have tea? Coffee? We've got all three."

"Lemonade is fine, thanks. Hi, everyone."

Lenora was sitting on the sofa, her knitting basket beside her. She looked up from the blue scarf she was working on for her grandson in Alabama. "Come sit by me." She moved her basket to one side. "I've been thinking about you all day."

"Aw, that's sweet." Savannah sat down and rested her head against Lenora's shoulder for a couple of seconds.

"You doing okay, sugar? It's been a tough day, hasn't it?"

"Savannah has had a tough week," Jillian said.

"That I have, but you ladies have made it bearable." Savannah's gaze fell on cookware, dishes, and stack of books on the coffee table. "Miss Rita's bequests to you?"

"Yes, indeed," Bertie said. "You just missed Gary Moody. He stopped by and dropped these things off."

"He didn't stay long," Cornelia said, returning with a glass of lemonade. "I think he thought we'd start bothering him about that Vinton woman. And I would've, if he'd stayed long enough."

"Yes, and he knew it too." Bertie held out a plate of sugar cookies. "Here, Savannah. Have one of these. They're Lenora's own recipe."

"Oh, I love those. Thank you." She took two and bit into one. "I'm worn down to a nub, but I wanted to tell you about this afternoon."

"What about it?" Jillian said.

"For one thing, I went to the sheriff's office after I left the bakery."

"Mercy," Cornelia said as she handed her the icy glass of lemonade. "Something happen?"

"I wanted to let them know who owned the stuff in the lockbox." She paused. "I assume Jillian filled you in about that?"

"She did," Bertie said. "I've always liked Stewie."

"He lives such a simple life, I imagine he thought he wouldn't have any use for that money," Cornelia added. "As I remember, he and Jenny never did go in for a lot of fuss and feathers."

"So did you talk to Coy?" Lenora was never one to beat around the bush.

"I did. And he told me something quite interesting."

Cornelia sat down in her favorite chair, her back straight, her eyes bright. "We're all ears."

"Apparently Sheriff Pointer was just as crooked as Stewie thought."

"I remember he wasn't in office very long," Bertie said. "And there was plenty of talk about him while he was."

"What'd he do?" Jillian asked.

Savannah took a sip from her glass before continuing. "You know Sheriff Henderson isn't going to share a lot of information, but he did say any and all reports that were filed with the county back then were destroyed before Pointer left office."

"What?" Jillian said. "You mean Pointer got rid of them?"

"There was a fire," Savannah said as she put her glass on a coaster. "And there was no way to prove who set it, but the sheriff seems pretty convinced Pointer did it or hired it done."

"But why?" Cornelia scanned the small group as if she thought one of them had the answer.

"I imagine he was responsible for some of the criminal activity he refused to report," Bertie said.

"Makes sense to me," Lenora added. "Didn't he hightail it out of here soon after he left office?"

Savannah nodded. "Henderson said he took off for parts unknown, and he has no idea where he is to this day. But he figures he probably had something to do with the theft at Stewie's and other places. And even if he didn't, Stewie's report was destroyed, and it's unlikely there was ever an investigation."

"Did you tell Boone?" Bertie asked.

"I went by Food for Less, but he looked really busy. I didn't want to disturb him, nor did he seem like he wanted to be disturbed. I'll talk to him another time."

"Let me tell you ladies something. That boy is peculiar," Cornelia said. "Any time I've been around him, he hardly says two words, but when he was here for supper the other night, he talked our ears off. Didn't he, girls?"

"He was chatty, for sure," Jillian said. "He had a lot of interesting things to say."

"He's a deep thinker, I believe," Bertie said. "The quiet ones usually are."

"And it's the quiet ones that are the most peculiar," Cornelia insisted.

Jillian decided not to respond to that comment.

"Well, he's going through a lot himself," Lenora said. "Cut him some slack."

"I'm as slack as I can be." Cornelia's face took on an indignant expression. "I sent most of those cookies home with him, didn't I, Bertie?"

"Yes, Cornelia." Bertie sighed. "There is no disputing that you did send home a bunch of cookies with Boone. And the rest of the buttermilk pie. And a quart of that applesauce. And a jar of pickles."

"Just as long as you remember that and don't accuse me of maligning his character when I say he's peculiar. Peculiar isn't a dirty word. It's a character trait."

Bertie muttered something that Jillian chose not to hear. Her grandmother and great-aunt frequently bickered like little girls, and while their fussing occasionally entertained her, today was not one of those days.

Savannah opened her oversize purse. "I met Gary Moody at the bank early this afternoon, and we got into the safe-deposit box that held items Miss Rita left for me. I thought you might like to see what they are."

"We sure would." Lenora leaned forward eagerly.

First, Savannah pulled out a large manila envelope. Next, she withdrew a plain white business envelope, and finally, a paper vellum square.

"None of them look like they've ever been opened. Haven't you gone through any of this?" Jillian asked.

Savannah shook her head. "I have no idea what I'm going to find, and to tell you the truth, I simply wanted my friends with me when I see what's inside. I wish James were here."

"Well, honey, we're here for you now," Lenora said. "And I sincerely doubt you will find anything but good in whatever Miss Rita has left you."

"You're right, of course, but it's just been such a stressful time." She gave them all a grateful smile. "Thank you for being such loyal friends."

"Don't you go making us cry, child," Lenora said brusquely. "Now, let's see what's in those envelopes."

Everyone scooched around in the chairs, giving her and the parcels in her hands their full attention.

Savannah picked up the vellum square and carefully broke the seal. "It's pictures," she said with a smile.

"Why would anyone keep pictures in a safe-deposit box?" Cornelia's face creased in puzzlement.

"Because they don't want to lose them," Bertie said. "Some photos can't be replaced."

"That makes sense. Do we have our photos in a box at the bank?"

"No, Cornelia, but they're in a safe place."

"I think you should put them in the bank. What if someone broke into Belle Haven and swiped all our family pictures?"

"Goodness me, Cornelia, why would anyone but family want pictures of us? Anyway, last time we had them out, I decided they needed to be in a better place than old shoe boxes. I bought a fireproof box that even locks and put them inside it, so stop fretting."

Cornelia pondered for a minute, then nodded and said nothing more.

Savannah studied the photos in her hand, her expression soft, her mouth curved up in a gentle smile. "I think these are snaps of Miss Rita when she was young, but I'm not sure."

Bertie held out a hand. "Let me see, honey. I can tell." She eyed the photos. "That's her, sure enough. She was a pretty little thing."

"Let me see." Cornelia held out her hand, and Bertie passed them on.

"These must be Ryan's school photos." Savannah smiled at the pictures in her hand. "He was a cute little kid who grew into a handsome teenager." She handed them to Bertie as she finished with each. "Here he is in a soldier's uniform. And one of him and another soldier. And him and a girl with long hair and bangs. That's all the pictures there are."

Jillian thumbed through the photos when they reached her. She studied the picture of Ryan and the second soldier. Both of them were holding half-smoked cigarettes and they had their caps pushed back, grinning into the camera lens. She flipped the photo over.

"The back says, 'Ryan and Sonny, 1972.'" She glanced at the backs of the others. Each school photo had the year recorded, and the picture of him and the dark-haired girl read *Ryan and Janine*. "'Ryan and Janine.' I've heard that name before."

"Boone's girlfriend," Cornelia said. She frowned. "No, that was Regina."

"No, you were right the first time, Aunt Cornelia. He said something about he and Janine breaking up after Ryan got back from Vietnam. And now we know why." Jillian waved the photo, then placed all of them on the table as Savannah began pulling papers from the business envelope.

She gasped, her eyes widening. "These are two $1,000 certificates of deposit in my name. Apparently Miss Rita had them set up several years ago."

Lenora gaped at the money. "Bless her heart."

"Absolutely, bless her heart, thinking of me in this way." Savannah shook her head. "I don't know what to say." She stared at them with wide eyes.

"You let your heart say thank you," Bertie said. "When you pray, offer a prayer of gratitude."

"And do something good for someone else." Cornelia gave her an encouraging smile. "When someone does something good for others, just think how the world brightens up. If we all did it more often, why, just think how much happier folks would be everywhere."

Savannah went to Cornelia and kissed her cheek. "Thank you for that reminder."

"We all need to remember that," Jillian said.

"That we do." Bertie nodded enthusiastically. "My little sister is flaky sometimes, but she can be quite wise."

To Jillian's surprise, Cornelia let the "flaky" dig go by without comment and sat down in her usual chair. She picked up her tatting shuttle and thread, but her hands remained idle.

"Did you go see Pastor Julie yet?" Jillian asked Savannah.

"I did."

"What did she say when you gave her that check?"

"She was grateful. And speechless for a bit. Then she said that with the donation the church had received from Boone that day and what Stewie and I gave, they would get some new plumbing and a new roof."

"Boone gave something too?"

Savannah nodded, smiling. "In memory of Miss Rita."

"I declare." Cornelia beamed. "I knew that boy had a good heart."

"Even as peculiar as he is?"

"Hush that kind of sass, Jillian, or you can go to your room."

"I'm not ten years old anymore." Jillian settled back in her seat.

Savannah replaced the certificates of deposit, then picked up the manila envelope. She studied it thoughtfully for a few seconds before unfastening the brass clasp and shaking out the contents onto her lap: two more envelopes and a folded piece of paper.

She picked up the document folded lengthwise in thirds and opened it.

"A marriage license?" Lenora leaned in, straining to read.

"Yes. And get this—the names are Ryan Mitchell Carter and Janine Lee Morrow."

Jillian blinked in surprise. "They were married? Why didn't Miss Rita tell us?"

Savannah shook her head. "This isn't signed. They weren't married."

"Maybe there's a signed one in with all that." Cornelia dipped her head toward the two unopened envelopes in Savannah's lap.

"Maybe." Savannah picked one up and read the front of it. "Oh my. Jillian, look at whose name is on this." She held it out so Jillian could see the words.

Allison Vinton only.

"Open it," Lenora said, putting aside her knitting.

Savannah shook her head. "I'm not going to open it. It says 'Allison Vinton only.' I am not included in that."

"But Miss Rita left you the contents of that safe-deposit box," Cornelia pointed out. "Everything in it is legally yours."

"That doesn't mean she wants me to read something clearly marked for someone else."

"But you don't know this Vinton person." Cornelia paused and blinked, as though listening to the echo of her words. "I wonder what Raymond thinks about all this." She glanced around. "Possum? Now where did he go? He was here just a minute ago. Here, kitty, kitty." She got up and scurried out of the room, calling for the cat.

"Who is the other envelope addressed to?" Jillian asked.

Savannah picked it up. "Oh, it's for me."

"Good." Jillian felt a wave of relief. "Maybe it will explain a few things."

"I hope so," Savannah said fervently. "These little secrets are making me jumpy."

She opened the sealed flap and pulled out one page, penned in Miss Rita's neat, precise handwriting. She read silently while the others watched and waited.

"Can you share what you just read? Or is it confidential?" Jillian thought if one more bit of information was termed confidential, she might scream.

Savannah lifted her head. "Basically, Miss Rita asks me to try to find Allison Vinton. She says to get you to help me because, as she phrases it here, 'Jillian is so good at getting to the bottom of things.'"

"What does that mean?"

"I think she meant you have good instincts and imagination, and can see past obstacles."

"I do?"

"Of course you do, honey," Bertie said. "I have full faith in you, and obviously so do many other people, Miss Rita included."

"Oh." Jillian wrinkled her nose. "But Gary Moody has already found her, and she wants to stay hidden."

"I suppose Miss Rita was just covering all bases, making sure the woman was found." Savannah murmured.

Jillian thought for a moment. "I think the only thing to do now is to march that letter down to Gary Moody."

Jillian and Savannah used their lunch break the next day to go to the law office. Gary Moody was just coming out the door as they arrived, chatting on his cell phone. He walked past them with barely a nod, then paused and faced them. "Are you here to see me?"

"Yes please," Savannah said. "It won't take long."

A frown skittered across his face, then he muttered into the phone and disconnected the call. "I only have a minute."

"This was in the safe-deposit box yesterday, and I thought you should see it." Savannah held out the letter Miss Rita had written to her.

Gary made a show of examining his watch, then took the letter and read it quickly. He handed it back.

"So how can I reach Ms. Vinton?" Savannah asked.

He gave her a slight smile. "I'm not breaching her confidentiality, Savannah. I'll tell her about Miss Rita's wishes, and if Ms. Vinton wants to contact you, she will."

"But it's Miss Rita's request."

"Sorry, but Ms. Vinton wants everything to go through me for now. Excuse me, please. I have to be in court. Good afternoon, Savannah. Jillian."

Jillian put up a hand. "But, Gary, can't you just—"

He got into his black BMW, closed the door, and started the engine. A few seconds later, he pulled out of his parking space and drove away.

"Well, how do you like that?" Jillian clenched her hands so tightly they turned white.

Savannah glared at the car as it disappeared down the street. "I hate to sound bitter, but ever since he started practicing law, Gary Moody has acted too big for his britches. I remember when he was a skinny carryout boy at the grocery store." She blew out a deep breath. "But, as you said yesterday, he has rules and regulations, and it's best if I remind myself of them." She met Jillian's eyes. "Otherwise, I might get downright mad at him."

For the next week, Jillian was busy at the bakery and Savannah spent her time catching up on the accounting work she'd let slide for the last little while. Although Hunter had returned from his trip to Alabama in time to help coordinate Miss Rita's funeral service, he and Jillian had seen little of each other apart from him dropping by the bakery occasionally for a midday coffee. They finally had time for a dinner date at Crazy Fish Bar & Grill Thursday night, and it was just as Jillian was walking inside Belle Haven after Hunter had walked her to the door that Savannah called her.

"I got word that Boone is going to start packing up Miss Rita's things," Savannah said by way of greeting. "I was wondering if you can get away from the bakery and go with me Saturday morning to help him."

Jillian hoped taking more time off wouldn't cause her grandmother and Lenora any problems. So far, however, anything having to do with Miss Rita had gotten a pass from the pair. "I'll be happy to."

"I'll pick you up bright and early."

"Is James going to help?"

"Are you kidding?" Savannah laughed. "He and all those men are going to be elbow deep in fixing up Cherry in Larry Don's shop. James has spent every free minute over there, even when he had that rotten bug."

"You *named* the car?"

"James did. He calls her Cherry Baby."

"Oh, good grief."

"I know, right? I can't help but giggle at him, and he just looks at me as if I'm the one who's being silly."

"Well, Savannah, you just referred to it as 'her' and as 'Cherry.'"

There was a brief silence, then Savannah burst out laughing. "I did, didn't I? You know that old saying, 'If you can't beat 'em, join 'em.' Not that there's anything to beat. Oh, and I found a small company that reupholsters car interiors. We'll be talking to them soon."

Jillian could hear the smile in her friend's voice and was so glad she could. Savannah needed to smile and to laugh these days. They chatted a few more minutes, then ended the call.

Savannah showed up at Belle Haven Saturday morning at eight o'clock to pick Jillian up. When Bertie found out Savannah planned to help pack up Miss Rita's belongings, she was more than happy that Jillian would be helping.

"Going through a deceased loved one's belongings is dreadful at the worst and bittersweet at the best. Boone and Savannah need you far more than The Chocolate Shoppe does today."

"Good gracious, yes," Cornelia added. "I can always fill in for you, Jillian."

Jillian's heart flooded with gratitude and love for her grandmother and great-aunt. No one could be any more blessed with family.

That morning, Savannah wore her hair in a neat ponytail and was dressed in denim shorts and a much-worn T-shirt. She eyed Jillian's attire, which was much the same with one exception. "If I were you, I'd wear sneakers instead of sandals."

Jillian stuck out one foot. "But I just painted my toenails this new color in honor of your car and I want to admire it. It's called Cherry-Berry Cooler."

"Very nice. But what if you drop something heavy on your foot?"

She grimaced. "Are you saying I'm accident-prone? I might drop an iron skillet on my foot in the mornings while I'm frying pancakes, but that doesn't mean I'm going to wear combat boots to cook breakfast."

Savannah hooted with laughter. "I'll wait while you grab a change of shoes."

"You sure are bossy," Jillian grumbled good-naturedly as she left the room.

They arrived at Miss Rita's house a short while later. Savannah's gaze scoured the yard and front porch as she got out of the car. "I wonder where Boone is."

"Maybe he had to work last night," Jillian said.

"Maybe. We can get started anyway." Savannah pulled a key from her pocket as they ascended the porch steps.

"You have a key to the front door?"

"Don't sound so scandalized, Jillian. I've had one for years. I'll give it to Boone when we're finished today, but it's lucky I have it now, isn't it?" She started to insert the key into the front door lock, but the door swung open at her touch.

They froze and stared at each other with wide eyes.

"I guess you don't need that key," Jillian whispered.

Savannah nodded and pushed the door open. They stood on the threshold, gazing in.

"I think Boone must have forgotten to lock up." Savannah stepped inside and Jillian followed. The living room was just as it always had been, and there was the usual slight scent of lemon oil in the air. "I guess he hasn't started packing yet."

They walked to the kitchen and stopped abruptly when they

were met with complete disarray, counters piled high, cabinet doors open.

"My goodness!" Savannah gasped. "Why is it like this?"

"Do you suppose someone broke in?" Jillian whispered. "After all, it's common knowledge that Miss Rita is gone."

Savannah caught Jillian's hand and pulled her along as she moved through the kitchen, noting the empty cabinets, the canned goods and boxes lying helter-skelter.

"Boone will have a fit when he sees this," Savannah said. "He's always so tidy and organized."

They stepped into a hallway off the kitchen and Savannah halted, her grip tightening. "Look at that."

The hallway was clogged with clothes, shoes, books, and more. As they stared at it, there was a loud thump in the bedroom at the end of the hall.

"Who's here?" Jillian called out.

Something thumped, then crashed. A moment later, Boone stepped out of the room. His white hair was disheveled, his face flushed, his clothing sweat-stained and wrinkled.

"Boone, what happened? Did someone break in and ransack the place?"

"What are you doing here?" he growled.

"We came to help," Savannah said, sounding as bewildered as Jillian felt. "Packing up and disposing of everything in this house is a big job."

"I'm handling it."

"What happened? Who did this?" Savannah asked.

"I'm going through her things. I'm in the sorting stage right now."

Sorting? Jillian grimaced. How could any of that conglomeration tossed willy-nilly be considered sorted?

Savannah eyed the heaps that surrounded them. She was

obviously sharing Jillian's thoughts. She straightened her shoulders and gave a smile. "Well, we're here to help you and make this job—"

"No need." He shook his head and stepped over a few mountains to reach them. "I'm getting along just fine."

"But Boone, this is going to take forever. The three of us can get it done a lot quicker." Savannah appraised him quickly. "You've been at this all night, haven't you? You're still in your Food for Less clothes."

He ran both hands through his hair, exaggerating its disarray. Something seemed to go out of him and he deflated, exhaustion taking over his features. "I came over when I got off work to formulate some kind of plan for packing it up and distributing everything, and . . ."

"And you didn't go home, did you?" Jillian asked.

He shook his head.

"Well, then, it's time you took a break. I'm sure I can whip us up a breakfast here."

"No thanks, Jillian."

"Oh, but—"

"No thank you." His gaze pierced her. "I want to do this alone. I need to."

Savannah started forward. "But—"

He glared at Savannah, who stopped short. "It might sound crazy to you, but I don't care. This is my chance to tell her goodbye, and I want to do it alone."

"It will take you a long time."

"Not if you leave now and let me get on with it. I plan to set out plenty of keepsakes for her friends to take, and the rest will go to charity." He left it at that and simply watched them, waiting for them to leave.

"I guess we should go," Savannah said quietly to Jillian.

"I guess so." How would he get through that mess by himself? Jillian dared not ask, but she wondered.

Savannah put a hand on Boone's arm. "If you change your mind, call me."

"I won't change it."

"But if you do, my number is on that list on Miss Rita's fridge."

"I know."

They stood a moment longer. Perhaps a moment too long, because he narrowed his eyes. "Goodbye."

Once in the car, Savannah released a frustrated breath. "I don't feel good about this. He should not be bearing this load by himself. Did you see his face, his eyes? He's not a young man. What if he collapses in there, alone?"

Jillian shook her head gently. "Sometimes things have to be taken on faith."

"I know, but that doesn't change the fact that he's bereaved, he's alone, and he has a huge job ahead of him. And he's probably confused."

"Why would he be confused?"

"Because that house has been left to a total stranger. Don't you think he's racking his brain, trying to figure out who Allison Vinton is and why she now owns Miss Rita's property?"

"Maybe he knows her."

Savannah stared at Jillian as if she'd lost her senses. "How in the world would he know her?"

"Well, think about it. All these years, he and Miss Rita have been as close as can be. Allison Vinton was important enough to her that she left her house to the woman, so it seems likely that Boone knows her, even though he said he didn't."

"If this has been in your head all this time, why on earth didn't you bring it up before now? Why didn't you ask Boone?"

"I just thought of it," Jillian protested.

Savannah blew out an exasperated huff of air. "Sometimes, Jillian Green, you beat everything. You know that?"

Jillian gave her a beatific smile. "Yes, I know. That's why we're best friends."

"Oh, brother," Savannah muttered. She started the engine. "Well, if we can't do anything here, let's go see the progress on Cherry. After all, the guys did promise Miss Rita they would teach me about car maintenance."

"Okay. Just think, you'll have all the rest of this beautiful Saturday to be crawling around under an old car. All I have to do is get back to the bakery and shape dinner rolls."

A couple of blocks away, in Larry Don Benning's garage, they found James, Larry Don, Gooder, and Hugh Honeycutt. Engine parts and tools lay on the floor, and the men were happily at work on the engine. Nearby were a stack of paper to-go cups, two huge insulated jugs of coffee, and two boxes of various doughnuts from The Chocolate Shoppe.

"You're at it bright and early," Jillian called out as they approached the car.

Larry Don rolled out from under the carriage, and the other three straightened and faced the women. Already their clothes were filthy and their hands dark with dirt and oil.

"Good morning, ladies," Hugh said. "Y'all here to help?"

"Not if I have to get that dirty," Jillian said. "Hunter won't keep his word to take me dining and dancing at the swankiest place in town tonight if he sees me like that."

"I doubt that. How do you know he wouldn't like you even more for being willing to get your hands dirty?" Savannah stepped up to the car and studied the engine as if she understood every nut, bolt, and wire in it.

"James said you two were gonna help Boone pack up Miss Rita's house this morning," Larry Don said as he got to his feet. He wiped his hands on a grimy rag.

"Boone wants to do it by himself," Savannah said as she

leaned closer to the engine. "Is that carburetor going to have to be replaced?"

Hugh glanced at her in surprise. "Most likely. You know much about cars?"

"Not a whole lot, but some. James has been teaching me a bit."

"Good. I wish Maudie would learn a few things about her car. What'll she do if something happens to me?"

"We'll take care of her," Savannah said, "but let's hope nothing happens to you for a good long time, Hugh. We like having you around."

"Why, thank you for saying so. I plan to be here for a while yet." He grinned at her. "So tell me, why does Boone want to do that job by himself? Seems to me like he'd appreciate having a couple of pretty girls around."

"Boone is antisocial." Larry Don came up behind them and peered at the engine as if searching for something he hadn't seen yet. "He doesn't like anyone, and he never has."

Savannah frowned. "I don't believe that for a minute."

"He loved Miss Rita," Jillian said.

Larry Don made a face. "Well, yeah, her. But that's all."

Jillian crossed her arms. "He was mighty nice to us when he came for dinner."

Larry Don blinked in surprise. "He actually went to Belle Haven?"

"He did. Shortly before Miss Rita passed away. We had a wonderful visit."

"You did?" Larry Don's expression said he didn't believe it. "Well, tell me, Jillian, has he ever said anything to you about what he's going to do with all that old junk in Miss Rita's house? I mean, if he wants to get rid of it, I'll cart it off for him."

Savannah glowered at him. "Kindly do not call Miss Rita's belongings 'old junk.'"

"I'm sure she has a few collectibles in there that will bring him a pretty penny," Larry Don said, rubbing his hands on the rag again. "Like as not, he doesn't want you in there laying claim to any of it."

"Is that why you're so eager to 'cart it off' for him?" Jillian did not try to mask her irritation.

He scowled. "Now that's uncalled for, Jillian. I'm just trying to be a good neighbor."

Savannah found her voice and her backbone. "You are getting well-paid to restore a car, Larry Don, and it would behoove you to know we're letting you restore it because that's what Miss Rita wanted us to do."

His face darkened. "Now see here—"

"Let's go, Jillian," Savannah snapped, whirling on her heel and storming out. "You're needed at the bakery."

"Honey?" James followed them out of the garage. Concern lay across his usually placid features. "Are you okay?"

"I'm too aggravated right now to talk," she said. She kissed his cheek lightly. "I'll see you tonight." She glanced beyond him, into the interior of the mechanic shop. "And watch out for that Larry Don. I don't trust him."

The regular Sunday afternoon gathering of the Southern Sweetie Pies was in full swing at the bakery when Savannah's cell phone rang. She excused herself from the group and went into the kitchen before she answered.

A minute later, she returned and tapped Jillian on the shoulder. She hissed in her ear, "We're needed over at Miss Rita's. Let's go."

Jillian trusted her friend and knew she wouldn't be calling her away from the meeting unless something important, even urgent, had occurred. She caught Bertie's eyes and signaled to her. Her grandmother nodded, and the two hustled away, ignoring the questions from the other Sweetie Pies.

"What's going on?" Jillian asked the moment they were outside.

"That was Boone on the phone. He asked if we could get over there ASAP."

"Why?"

"He didn't say. His calling for help is enough for me to know it's urgent."

They arrived at Miss Rita's house a short time later and were surprised to see a new white Cadillac in the driveway. Boone's pickup was backed up to the shed and the shed doors were wide open, revealing an empty building.

"I wonder who that is." Savannah pointed toward the white car. "Does Larry Don have a new Caddy?"

Jillian shrugged. "He might. I hope he's not in there bothering Boone."

"I guess we'll find out soon enough."

Jillian peered closer at the car. "Those aren't Georgia plates. That car is from Arkansas."

"So it is." They climbed the steps, but Savannah paused at the door. She spoke in an undertone. "I hear a woman's voice."

"So do I. I wonder who it is."

Savannah knocked, and conversation inside the house stopped as quick footsteps approached. A slender, middle-aged woman with sleek dark hair in a chin-length bob appeared at the door. She neither smiled nor spoke, but opened the door and indicated that they should enter. Jillian was so surprised by her presence, she forgot to greet the woman.

Boone stood in the middle of the living room, his body tense, his face hard. "Hello, Savannah, Jillian. Have a seat."

"Please do," the woman said, her tone cool and clipped.

They sat side by side on the edge of the sofa. Jillian knew Savannah was as edgy and bewildered as she was. Boone said nothing.

"What's this about?" Savannah asked. "Who are you?"

The woman sank gracefully into a wing chair, her tailored pearl-gray suit fitting her frame perfectly. Her tapered-toe, black high heels seemed almost lethal in their sharp design. "I am Allison Vinton."

"Oh!" Savannah's voice was little more than a squeak. She cleared her throat, and the smile she offered looked painfully forced. "How do you do? I'm Savannah Cantrell and—"

"Introductions are unnecessary, as is your presence here. I know who you are, and I realize you have a vested interest in this property." She passed a gaze to each one in turn. "I am sure you realize why I'm here."

Boone's facial muscles worked, but he still said nothing.

Ms. Vinton spoke again. "For the life of me, I cannot understand why some elderly woman I never knew existed willed me an old house."

"Didn't Gary Moody tell you the details?" Savannah asked.

The woman uttered a humorless laugh. "I got the distinct impression he does not know the details behind this bequest, nor does he care. Apparently his job is done." She pinned a hard glare on Savannah. "Mr. Hackett doesn't know why the place is mine now either. Perhaps you would care to enlighten me."

"Me? I'm just as bewildered as you are."

"Bewildered does not begin to describe how I feel." Ms. Vinton sniffed and straightened her straight spine even more. "I understand from Mr. Moody that you have a letter for me from this Carter woman."

"I do, but it's at home."

Ms. Vinton blinked at her. "You didn't bring it?"

"I had no idea you were here."

"I thought that's why he called you." She transferred her accusing eyes to Boone. "You didn't tell her to bring the letter that woman left for me?"

He scowled. "Would you please stop referring to her as 'that woman'? Her name was Miss Rita."

Her face creased in a frown, Savannah pulled her phone from her purse and tapped a number. A few moments later she said, "Hi, James. Would you do me a favor and run over to my place and get those letters from Miss Rita? They're in my rolltop desk. Bring both of them over to her house, please. Thanks, honey." She ended the call and met Ms. Vinton's eyes. "I'll have the letter for you soon."

The woman favored her with a single cold nod.

An uncomfortable silence fell over them, which Jillian finally broke by asking Savannah, "Are the guys working on Cherry this afternoon?"

"Of course. You know they're going to work on her every free moment."

"I've never seen guys get so grimy as fast as they did yesterday."

"From head to foot. It's a wonder that gunk washes off."

Ms. Vinton glanced back and forth between them, mild curiosity flickering across her face, but neither Savannah nor Jillian explained Cherry to her. Instead, Savannah turned to Boone, who had been studying his hands linked together in his lap. "Are you going to work on Cherry?"

He shrugged. "Maybe if I get some time."

"Have you made much headway in your sorting and packing?"

"Yeah, some. Want me to show you?"

She smiled at him. "Sure."

Savannah and Jillian went with him and saw that he had indeed made considerable progress. The hallway had been cleared except for a couple of large, black trash bags at the far end. He led them into the spare room, where the bed had been dismantled and parts were leaning against one wall. Several boxes were stacked in neat sections in the area that was free of furniture.

"Items in the boxes on that side are going to be divided between the Heart for Home Charity Shop and Cause for Paws Thrift Store," Boone explained. He pointed to another area. "The boxes in that corner are where I'm putting keepsakes for folks who might want something of Miss Rita's to remember her by. Jillian, if you want more of her books, or if you think Miss Cornelia or Miss Bertie might like to have them, I'll be packing them in these boxes here." He indicated the empty cartons near the door.

"Thank you so much." Jillian smiled at him but figured the overfull shelves in the library at Belle Haven would sag if she added to them. On the other hand, in her estimation, no one could ever have too many books.

"Are you going to get everything out of here by the end of the week?" Ms. Vinton spoke right behind them. "Because if you aren't, I'll have to charge you storage costs for every day beyond Saturday."

All three faced her, eyes wide. The woman stood with arms crossed, her stern features icy.

"I don't think that's legal," Savannah said.

The woman gave her a tight smile. "Oh, it's completely legal, I assure you. I am in property development and management, so I know what I'm doing. And if there is any dispute, I have Mr. Hackett's signature on an agreement to have everything cleared out by then."

Savannah whirled toward Boone. "Is that true?"

"Gary Moody drew one up," he muttered.

"And you signed it?"

He nodded.

"Oh, Boone." Savannah's voice filled with despair. "I wish you had talked to me—"

"Why are you trying to make this situation more difficult than it needs to be?" Ms. Vinton asked. "This house is my property now, and I'm perfectly within my rights to ask that all things belonging to someone else be removed."

"You might be perfectly within your rights," Jillian said with heat, "but I see no reason for you to be so hasty and pressure Boone like this. Do you realize what an undertaking it is to clear out—"

"Spare me whatever sob story you were planning to share. I've dealt with houses belonging to 'dear old Grandma' before." Vitriol seemed to fuel Ms. Vinton's fingers as she made air quotes. "I am perfectly happy to take over the disposal of all this stuff if it's too much for Mr. Hackett to handle. Having no attachment to it, I can get the place cleaned out in short order and save us all a lot of time and trouble."

As Ms. Vinton spoke, Jillian curled her hands into fists, tightly enough that her nails bit painfully into the flesh of her palms. She struggled to keep calm and swallowed the harsh words that fought for release.

"We are here to help him, if he wants our help," Savannah said quietly. "We'll be happy to take care of this, so you needn't bother yourself with it, Ms. Vinton."

Why on earth had Miss Rita left such a significant legacy to this iceberg of a woman? What possible connection could have ever been between the two of them? This was the time to figure it out—*if I can keep my cool and ask the right questions.*

"Why don't we go into the front room and have coffee while we wait for James?" she suggested. Maybe the atmosphere of shared coffee would nurture a little calm and reason into the situation and give them an opportunity to learn something about this woman.

"Good idea," Boone said. "I'll make it."

"Fine." Ms. Vinton pivoted sharply and led the way back to the living room while Boone went into the kitchen.

"Where do you live, Ms. Vinton?" Jillian sat down on the sofa and plastered as much interest on her face as she could feign. She even managed to force a smile.

"Little Rock." Ms. Vinton settled into an armchair.

"My, that's quite a way from Moss Hollow."

"Yes, it is. And I really don't have time to be dealing with this situation."

"Couldn't you have dealt with it long distance?" The words were out before Jillian had taken time to consider them.

"Long distance? No. Some things in life can be handled somewhat blindly, I suppose, but real estate should never be one of them."

"I see." Although she didn't, really, especially given the fact that Ms. Vinton seemed resentful of the bequest. Jillian was missing a key element that was apparently obvious to the other woman.

After another minute, Ms. Vinton got up and strode to the front window. She glanced up and down the street, tapping her foot. "When will the man be here with that letter?"

"It won't be long," Savannah said. "But he does have to drive over to my house and then back across town, so it'll take a short while."

Ms. Vinton eyed the street in both directions again, as if she didn't trust Savannah's words, then turned from the window. Her gaze went over the lines of the room, a calculating, critical gaze that undoubtedly did not see the charm of the decor, nor the warmth and welcome that Miss Rita had put into it. As Jillian watched her, something leapt into the woman's eyes and her cold demeanor changed in an instant.

"What time is it?" Ms. Vinton cried, staring around wildly like something trapped.

Jillian blinked in surprise at the shift in attitude and glanced at her watch. "Nearly three o'clock."

Ms. Vinton grabbed her purse and plucked her phone out of it. "Excuse me." She ran out the front door.

"What was that all about?" Savannah stared at the door. "She was upset."

"Very much so, it seems." Jillian got up and went to the window. Savannah joined her. On the far side of the yard, pacing back and forth near the sidewalk, Ms. Vinton talked on her phone, gesturing with her free hand. "She seems really worried."

"Jillian, look. She dropped her phone. And is she crying?"

Sure enough, Ms. Vinton had come to a complete standstill and now had her face buried in both hands. Her shoulders were rounded, and her body shook. Sunlight glinted dully off the screen of her phone, which had landed on the sidewalk. As unlikable as the woman was, Jillian refused to let her go through what seemed to be a difficult moment alone. She had to at least offer a kind hand.

"I'll go see if I can help her." Jillian hurried outside and nearly ran to the woman. "Ms. Vinton, what's wrong? Can I do something for you?"

Ms. Vinton continued to sob into her hands while Jillian stared at her, feeling helpless. Not knowing how the woman would react to being touched, she hesitantly put a comforting hand on her shoulder, felt the heat of her shaking body. Ms. Vinton neither leaned into her nor shrunk away.

"Let's get out of the sun. Come on. We'll find a place to sit down." Jillian glanced toward the house just as Savannah and Boone stepped out of the front door. "Would one of you get her a glass of cold water?" she called to them. Then she lowered her voice and said soothingly to the crying woman, "Come now. Let's go back to the house."

Ms. Vinton went with her, head down, still sobbing, and as compliant as a needy child. Savannah reached out and took her arm as they got to the door.

"Come inside." Savannah led her to the nearest chair and settled her in it. She pulled up an ottoman and sat close by. "Here's Boone with some cold water for you. And a damp cloth."

"Thank you." Ms. Vinton mopped her face with the cloth, then took the glass from Boone's hand and drained it so fast, Jillian feared it would make her ill. "Thank you," she said again, shakily, and handed the glass back.

Boone said nothing as he took a few steps back, eyes watchful.

Savannah fetched a box of tissues from the bathroom and gave them to her.

Ms. Vinton blotted her reddened eyes and wet face. "I must look a fright."

"Not at all," Savannah said as she hunkered down beside her. "Can we get you anything else?"

Ms. Vinton blew her nose and shook her head. "I don't know what it would be unless it's a cure for cancer."

The other three exchanged glances then stared at her.

"Say what?" Boone stepped closer, turning his head to favor his good ear.

Ms. Vinton swallowed hard and took a deep shuddering breath. "My mother has cancer." She gulped in more air. "And we're hoping for a miracle."

"Oh, dear." Savannah took one trembling hand and held it between both of hers.

"I'm so sorry to hear she's so ill," Jillian said.

"So am I." Boone drew up the wing chair and sat down, leaning forward, resting his elbows on his knees as he gazed at her. "That's what took my mama. And Miss Rita."

"Oh, is it?" Ms. Vinton squeaked. "I'm sorry." She grabbed several more tissues. "It's such a terrible disease, taking people from their loved ones far too early."

"Well, ma'am, I don't mean to be rude, so please excuse me for asking, but if your mama is so sick, why are you here?" Boone's blue eyes were as guileless as a confused child's.

Ms. Vinton blinked at him. "Because I had to be here to take care of this crazy situation. This whole business—the will, the contract Mr. Moody drew up—is so convoluted, I don't even want to talk about it."

Jillian said, "But surely extenuating circumstances would dictate—"

Ms. Vinton shook her head, and Jillian stopped. The suit-clad woman gave them a weak smile, her green eyes brimming. "I apologize for being so rude and coming across as uncaring. I'm not normally like that." She sniffled and wiped her nose. "Please forgive me."

"Why, of course," Savannah said warmly, just as Jillian expected her to. "We've all been short-tempered at one time or another." She shot a glance at Boone, who had the grace to blush and duck his head. "These last few weeks have been stressful on all of us, so we understand how you feel."

"Yes, we do," Jillian said. "Don't we, Boone?"

He nodded.

"Is your mother having treatments?" Savannah asked.

Ms. Vinton nodded. "I was calling to see how she's doing, but she wasn't feeling well enough to talk. The treatments are making her feel so sick she doesn't want to continue with them. We have a caregiver staying with us, and she says Mom just wants to let go and pass on. The thing is, her prognosis for recovery is really good, but she is so tired of being sick. Did Mrs. Carter have treatments?"

"No ma'am," Boone answered.

"But there was no cure for what ailed her," Jillian said.

"Oh dear." Ms. Vinton sniffed. "Mr. Moody said she was quite elderly."

"Ninety-one," Savannah said.

"Mama's in her mid-sixties. She has a lot of years left. Or could." A sob caught in Ms. Vinton's throat.

"I'm so sorry to hear about this," Savannah said.

"Is there anything we can do to help you feel better?" Jillian asked.

"I doubt I'll ever feel better." Ms. Vinton's voice broke.

"Yes, you will." Savannah patted her hand. "You just sit there and breathe easy for a bit."

"Have you eaten anything today, ma'am?" Boone asked. When Ms. Vinton shook her head, he said, "Well, one thing Miss Rita always said was, 'You can't face life on an empty stomach.' I have just the thing for you."

"Oh, please." She stretched out one hand. "I don't want to put you to any bother. And I'm not in the least hungry."

"I know." He gave her a slight smile and went to the kitchen.

Ms. Vinton bit her lip as she stared after him. "He really is a nice man, isn't he?"

"Yes, he is," Savannah replied. "He's very quiet and keeps to himself most of the time, but he has a good heart. He and Miss

Rita were as close to being mother and son as two unrelated people can be."

"Then why didn't she leave him this house? She's a perfect stranger to me, and yet here I am, the new owner of her property. I don't understand."

Jillian and Savannah exchanged a glance.

"No one understands," Jillian said.

Ms. Vinton sighed and balled the tissue in her hand. "Well, I certainly seemed to have stepped into something of a sticky wicket, haven't I? I suppose he resents me, and I can't blame him."

Savannah shook her head. "I don't think he resents you. I think he's just confused. We are all confused."

"Amen to that. I haven't the foggiest notion who this woman is, other than what tiny little bit I found on the Internet. I didn't even find her obituary."

"Oh? I'll find out about that and see if we can get it posted." Jillian made a mental note to mention it to Hunter.

Boone came back from the kitchen a short time later, rolling Miss Rita's tea cart ahead of him. On it was a tray containing a bowl of soup, a sandwich, a glass of milk, and a piece of cake.

"My goodness," Ms. Vinton said faintly, eyeing the spread. "I—that is, it's been so long since anyone has waited on me like this."

"The soup is some Miss Rita made," Boone said. "She always made a big pot of it and froze it in meal-size containers." He smiled at Jillian and Savannah. "You girls want some soup? There's plenty more."

Jillian loved Miss Rita's potato-and-leek soup, but shook her head. "Thanks, but none for me. The Southern Sweetie Pies met this afternoon, and we always have more treats to taste than a person needs in a month, let alone every week."

"That's the absolute truth," Savannah said. "But I wouldn't mind some coffee, if it's ready."

"Sure enough." He hurried back to the kitchen and returned shortly with cups of coffee for everyone.

After Ms. Vinton had polished off every morsel and drop Boone had given her, she sat back. "I didn't realize I was so hungry. That was delicious. Thank you." She gave Boone a smile that not only softened her grim face but also brought an unexpected light into her eyes.

Boone stared at her and sat down hard. All color drained from his face.

"Boone?" Jillian reached out one hand toward him.

17

Ms. Vinton regarded Boone in considerable alarm as he stared at her, white-faced and silent. She leaned forward. "What's wrong? Are you ill?"

"Who *are* you?" he whispered.

"Well, my goodness. I'm Allison Vinton. You know that."

He said nothing but never took his eyes off her.

She raised an eyebrow at Savannah and Jillian. "Does he have some kind of cognitive problem?"

Savannah shook her head. "Boone? What's going on?"

Footsteps on the porch interrupted the discussion. A couple of knocks sounded, and Savannah got to her feet just as the door opened.

"Hi, honey," James said as he and Hunter entered. "I hope these are what you wanted." He handed her both letters, kissed her cheek, greeted Boone and Jillian, and gave a polite nod to Ms. Vinton.

"Thank you, yes." She introduced both men to Ms. Vinton, adding, "Ms. Vinton is the new owner of Miss Rita's house."

Both men gave her a quick sharp appraisal and shook her hand.

"Are you from Moss Hollow?" Hunter asked.

"Little Rock."

"Are you thinking of moving here?" James tipped his head to one side and offered her a courteous smile.

"No. Not at all." Some of Ms. Vinton's chilly reserve had returned and she lifted one eyebrow at Savannah. "You have the letter for me?"

Savannah nodded. "Yes, and here's the letter I received at the same time. These were in a safe-deposit box at our local bank." She handed both to the woman.

Ms. Vinton read Savannah's letter quickly, laid it aside, and then tore open the sealed envelope bearing her name.

Hunter gave Jillian a smile then sat on the sofa. Although she would have preferred to sit next to him, she stayed where she was. He probably thought it curious to find her on an ottoman near a woman no one had met until that day.

"Boone, how are you doing?" James asked. If he noticed Boone's pallor and expression, he hid it well. "We thought you'd be helping work on Cherry."

"I've been tied up here, taking care of Miss Rita's things."

"That's quite a job. You know we'll be happy to pitch in and help in any way we can."

"We sure will," Hunter added. "I can haul stuff in my pickup."

Boone's smile came and left quickly. "I'll take you up on that. Sounds like I have to get out right soon."

"*What?*" Ms. Vinton leaped to her feet, staring at the letter in her hand. "No, this is all a lie! This is crazy." Everyone stared at her as she gaped at the letter. Outrage and disbelief colored her face and she shook her head. "I don't believe a word of this. Not. One. Word."

"What in the world has you so upset?" Jillian asked. "What did Miss Rita write?"

"Read it for yourself!" Ms. Vinton thrust the page into her hands and stalked away. She stood at the front room window and tapped one foot, arms folded tightly against her chest.

"Read it to us, Jillian," Savannah said.

"If you're going to read it aloud, then I'm going outside." Ms. Vinton rushed out the front door.

"Maybe I should go with her." Savannah cast a distressed glance toward the front yard. "Poor thing. She has been on a roller coaster today, hasn't she?"

"Let her be," James said. "She strikes me as wanting to be alone at the moment."

Savannah looked doubtful and crossed to the window. "I'll keep an eye on her, at least."

"Okay, if you think you should." James nodded to Jillian. "Go ahead, Jillian."

"It's dated June 29 of this year."

"That's about the time Miss Rita was diagnosed." Boone's voice was quiet and hoarse, as though he was choking back words.

Jillian began to read.

Dear Allison,

This is my fifth attempt at writing this letter, and I've decided to dispense with the drawn-out explanations, accounts, or theories as to events. After all, they change nothing while dredging up confusion and painful memories.

The first time I met your mother, she was a lovely, shy girl of barely eighteen with long brown curls and a dimple in her left cheek. She wore a skirt I deemed far too short, and she smelled of Heaven Scent perfume.

Jillian paused and stared at her friends, surprised. "She knew Ms. Vinton's mother."

"It would seem so," Hunter said.

Boone hung his head and sat that way, unmoving, staring at his closed hands as Jillian continued.

Although she was shy and immature, she was also intelligent, warm, and generous. She had an artistic nature, and her creativity led her into oil painting and needlework. In my bedroom, you will find a landscape she painted for me the one Christmas she visited here.

Boone shifted in his chair, but did not raise his eyes.

Other than the gifts I'm leaving to various friends in Moss Hollow, I am bequeathing all furnishing and accoutrements to my dear friend Boone Hackett, save that landscape. Without explanation, I have instructed him to leave it where it is. If you choose not to keep this early work of your mother's, you may donate it to the Moss Hollow Art Guild.

Jillian stopped again. "Do you know which painting she's talking about, Boone?"

He gave a short, quick nod without meeting anyone's gaze.

"Is this the mysterious letter that we've all been wondering about?" James said. "I don't see anything particularly momentous about it. Why didn't Miss Rita just leave Ms. Vinton that painting in the will like she left everyone else's bequest?"

"I have no idea, but be patient. I'm sure there's more," Savannah told him.

"Yes there is," Jillian said, frowning slightly. "Let me keep reading."

I am sure you are wondering why you have inherited a house from someone you don't know. I suppose you could say this house is my idea of recompense for something I should have done long ago.

Unease began to squirm in Jillian's stomach. "I'm not sure I want to read the rest of this."

"Shall I?" Hunter held out one hand and she gladly gave the letter to him. She sank down on the ottoman once more as he picked up where she had left off.

> *The moment Ryan brought her into our house, I saw what a sweet, naïve young girl she was, so very adoring of Ryan, and so very trusting. I should have warned her right then that Ryan was wild and headstrong, that he most surely would break her heart. I should have called her parents. I should have done something. But I didn't. He was my life, my reason for living, and whatever Ryan wanted was what I wanted for him. If you are a mother now, perhaps you will understand—*

"What's he doin' here?" Boone shouted suddenly, leaping to his feet. His blazing glare was fixed on someone in the front yard. Without warning he charged across the room and out of the house. The others jumped up to follow after him.

Larry Don Benning was standing next to Ms. Vinton, talking a mile a minute, gesturing toward the house with one hand, his slick salesman smile fixed in place.

"What are you doing here?" Boone approached with such a long, purposeful stride that Larry Don stepped back.

"What's your problem?" Larry Don said, sounding defensive. "I just dropped by to see how you're doing, Boone, and saw this lovely young woman standing out here in some distress. I offered her my hankie." At this point he pulled a wrinkled red bandanna from his hip pocket and held it out to her.

She took a hasty step backward.

"We're in the middle of business right now," Boone said. "So if you can just go along about your own." He jerked his head toward the street.

"I came to see what's holding up my partners. I've got Cherry up on the rack and—"

"We'll be back to the garage shortly," Hunter said.

Ms. Vinton spoke up. "He's asking me about buying Mrs. Carter's house."

Larry Don slapped his mouth closed as if he'd been caught red-handed and was at a loss for words. A couple of moments later, he said, "All right, then. Yes, I am interested in buying this house and flipping it. Or maybe making it into a rental—"

"Miss Rita's not cold in her grave yet, and we all know you've been slinking around before she was even gone," Boone yelled. "So you'd best just get on back to your garage. And don't come here again unless you're asked."

Larry Don stayed right where he was. Antagonism bristled from every pore in his body. "This isn't your property, Boone, and it never has been. You don't have the right to order me off."

Fists clenched, Boone rapidly closed the space between them.

Jillian tensed, knowing a fight was likely to break out.

James and Hunter rushed in before a punch was thrown. James grabbed Boone's arms, and Hunter got hold of Larry Don. The two furious men struggled, but Hunter and James were strong and determined to keep the two from reaching each other.

"What in the world is wrong with you?" Disgust and alarm were plain on Ms. Vinton's face. "Fighting over the estate of an old lady everyone seemed to love, especially you? Is this the way she wanted you to dispose of her property, Mr. Hackett?"

The men struggled a bit longer, grunting and huffing, then gradually stopped thrashing to stare at Ms. Vinton. It seemed a long minute before Boone released his anger. His rigid stance eased, and James let go of his arms, slowly, watchfully.

"Let me go, Hunter. I won't cause any trouble." Larry Don's voice was quiet and controlled. Hunter stepped back, and Larry

Don flexed his back and shoulders. "I didn't mean to upset you, ma'am. I'm just trying to make a living, and I heard the new owner was here."

"How'd you hear that?" Ms. Vinton asked. "No, never mind. It's unimportant. Can we discuss this another time? There are several issues I need to take care of first."

He gave her a quick, humble nod, then reached into his shirt pocket and brought out a business card. "Call me when you're ready, please."

She took the card and glanced at it. "All right. Now, good day to you. We have our own business to deal with."

"All right." Larry Don shot a glance at James and Hunter. "I'll see you back at the garage?"

"Maybe," James said coldly.

They watched as Larry Don headed down the sidewalk, back toward his place of business. As soon as he was out of sight, Ms. Vinton faced them, hands on her hips.

"Well, what do you think? Do you believe Mrs. Carter was my grandmother?"

A complete silence fell over the group. When a monarch butterfly flitted across the yard, Jillian fancied she could almost hear the beat of its wings. Then something snapped, and they all blinked at one another.

"Your grandmother?" Jillian and Savannah chorused.

"Why would you say that?" James wore his bewilderment like a confused puppy.

Ms. Vinton fixed an exasperated stare on Jillian. "Didn't you people read that letter?"

"We hadn't finished when Boone and Larry Don—"

"He hasn't been on my good list for a long time, and when I saw him out here talking to you, ma'am, something busted inside me." Boone shot a dirty glance down the street in the direction Larry Don had gone. "He's been cruisin' for a bruisin', as the saying goes, but honestly, I'd rather not be the one who gives it to him."

Ms. Vinton's cell phone chimed and she grabbed it out of her pocket. "Yes?"

"Let's go inside and give her privacy," Jillian suggested, then led the way back to the house.

Once inside, Hunter picked up the letter from the coffee table where he'd dropped it and continued reading it out loud.

> *When the pair came into the house one night, with a shiny new marriage license in your mother's hand and a huge smile on her face, my heart dropped. Not because I didn't want her as a daughter-in-law, but because I knew how unhappy she'd be married to my son. Two nights*

later, Ryan disappeared and her heart was broken. You see, she was expecting you by then. She didn't tell me so, but I am not blind. I wanted to offer her my home for as long as she wanted to live here, but she left too, and never returned.

I lost my son, my unborn grandchild, and a lovely young woman whom I would have treated as my own. But it was not in me to search for her. My longing was solely for my son, and my energy was focused on willing him to come home.

The search for Ryan was futile, of course. He wanted to be away from me as much as he wanted to run from the responsibilities of fatherhood. When he didn't even return for the car that he loved more than me, I knew he'd never come back. I ceased all searching and beat down all hope. I turned to my students, my church, and my community, doing my best to leave untouched the brokenness of my life.

A few days ago, when I received my diagnosis, one of the first things I did was hire a private investigator to search for Janine Morrow. What he found was Allison Vinton, the only child of Janine Morrow and Thad Vinton.

Boone jerked as if he'd been poked.
"Janine?" Jillian yelped.
Hunter kept reading.

Because I did not do what I should have done all those years ago, at least now I can pay some sort of recompense

to you, dear Allison. My home might not be worth much,
but it is yours, free and clear, to do with as you please.
May the end result give you joy.

Lovingly,

Rita Carter

"My word," Savannah said. "All this time and she never said a thing, she never let on. Did you know about any of this, Boone? Did she ever mention having a granddaughter?"

He shook his head. "Never."

Hunter studied Boone's face for a few seconds. "Did you have an inkling about the situation with Ryan?"

Boone shook his head again.

"Wait a second," Jillian said. "I just remembered something. That night you had dinner with Bertie, Aunt Cornelia, and me, someone mentioned that Janine was your girlfriend at one time."

"She was. Until Ryan came home." Pain filled his expression, and he dropped his gaze, avoiding eye contact.

"Oh." After a short silence, Jillian said softly, "So that's why you . . . well, it seemed you saw something familiar about Ms. Vinton a bit earlier."

"I thought I did when she smiled. But I didn't really believe it until this letter." Boone swiped the letter from Hunter's hand and shook the pages. "Miss Rita and I never talked about Janine, not even once. She knew Janine was my girl. She knew Ryan double-crossed me." Bitterness lay heavily in his tone. "Janine was a good girl, and he took advantage of her." He clenched his jaw. "Ryan only ever cared about Ryan."

Recalling Ms. Vinton's reaction to the letter, Jillian knew this was the first she'd heard this information. *No wonder she ran outside, away from everyone. I might have done the same.* "Did you ever try to find Janine after she left?" she asked.

Boone shook his head.

Jillian raised an eyebrow. "Did you think she'd gone with Ryan?"

Boone paused, then sighed. "I figured she went with him and Sonny. She was crazy about Ryan, but I didn't see her up and leaving her folks, but I guess she did. I don't know." He took in a deep breath and blew it out, then handed the letter to Savannah. "All I knew was that she wanted to be with him more than she wanted to be with me. I've never pushed myself on anyone, and I sure wasn't gonna push myself on Janine."

"Apparently she didn't stay with Ryan." Savannah consulted the letter again. "She married someone named Thad Vinton."

The front door opened and Ms. Vinton slipped in quietly. Everyone fell silent and turned to her. She was smiling, but shaky. "My mother is feeling better. Strong enough to call me. She's reconsidered her decision and will continue with the treatments." She gulped air, then flung out one hand as though reaching for something to grab. "I feel a little odd."

She swayed and Boone caught her before she toppled over. He settled her into a chair, peered closely at her chalky face. "Are you all right?"

She nodded. "Just relieved." She wiped her forehead with one shaking hand. "I seem to be causing everyone so much upset here."

"You have every right to feel faint, Ms. Vinton." Boone had yet to take his eyes off her face. "In your place, I'd feel the same."

"We all would," Hunter added.

She offered them a trembling smile. "Mom has a very good chance for survival now."

Boone exhaled and bowed his head. When he raised it again, Jillian saw tears in his eyes. "We were good friends, your mother and I. When you smile, you look so much like her."

Ms. Vinton regarded him seriously. "Why does Mrs. Carter think she's my grandmother? Mom has never mentioned her. Or her son."

"Miss Rita must have believed her son was your father, because she'd never purposefully tell a lie," Boone said.

"But Thad Vinton was my father. He and my mother married in the spring of 1972, and I was born the following year." Ms. Vinton leaned forward. "He died five years ago, and he was the only man in her life. They were devoted to each other." She sat back, her gaze resting on the letter Boone had laid on the coffee table. "I don't understand why Mrs. Carter alleges my father is Ryan Carter. I've never heard of him. She left this house to me in the mistaken belief she somehow owed something to Mom and me. But surely you see I can't accept it."

Boone sat on the edge of the nearest chair and leaned toward her. "Ma'am, I'm sorry to tell you this, but you haven't been told the truth. Your mother and I were dating during the spring of 1972, and when Ryan came home from Vietnam that summer, she started going out with him. They were together until he left in the fall of 1972."

Ms. Vinton gaped at him in horror. "No! I—I don't believe you!"

Boone gave Jillian a pleading look. "Please leave us to talk in private."

As much as she yearned to be a part of this unfolding scene, Jillian nodded. She led the way as she, Hunter, James, and Savannah quietly exited Miss Rita's home.

Monday morning at the bakery, Wanda Jean Maplewood beckoned Jillian over to where she and Maudie sat with coffee and sticky buns. "So what happened yesterday?" Wanda Jean asked.

Jillian blinked at her. "What do you mean?"

"Hugh said Larry Don left to go talk to that stranger Miss Rita gave her house to," Maudie said, "and when he came back, he was blowing steam to beat the band."

"Did Boone really try to beat him up? Imagine that—Boone Hackett beating up someone." Wanda Jean shook her head and placidly sipped her coffee.

Jillian stifled a sigh. "No one beat up anyone. And if Boone or Ms. Vinton wants anyone to know what happened yesterday, they can speak for themselves."

The two women gave her identical glowers. "I must say, Jillian Green, you can be the most exasperating woman," Maudie said.

She offered the two older women a mild smile and more coffee, but refused to share details of yesterday's meeting.

Stewie spoke up from his corner. "In all that clearing out of the property he's been doing, did Boone unearth any more stolen property?"

"You still got your hearing aids in, Stewie?" Maudie asked.

"Yep."

"You must have 'em turned up, if you can hear everything we say," Wanda Jean said.

"I don't want to hear everything you say. That's why I turn them down or take them out when y'all are in here. But I'm curious about if Boone's found anything else."

"If so, he hasn't mentioned it," Jillian told him.

"You expecting him to unearth bars of gold or something?" Wanda Jean asked.

Stewie favored her with a sneer and made a big show of removing his hearing aids. He unfolded that morning's Atlanta paper with considerable noise, shot a sly glance at the women, then lost himself in the news of the day. Jillian stifled a chuckle and went into the kitchen to check on a batch of cookies.

Around midafternoon, Boone came into The Chocolate Shoppe. He was neatly dressed in his work uniform and politely greeted the women. "May I speak with you privately, Jillian?"

Was there ever a time when Boone didn't want privacy or a quiet place to talk? "Sure thing. Come with me." Jillian led him back to the storeroom.

"Allison drove back to Little Rock last night," he said after glancing around to make sure they were alone, "and she's going to find out the truth concerning what was in the letter from Miss Rita."

"What do you think she'll learn?"

"Well, the truth, sooner or later. I hope it doesn't upset Janine, though. I reckon she's been through enough in her lifetime, and there's nothing in the world I have ever wanted more for that girl than to be happy."

Jillian touched his arm. "You still love Janine, don't you?"

He shifted from foot to foot. "There's never been anyone else."

"Are you going to see her again?"

Boone lifted his shoulders. "Aw, I don't know. She likely won't want to have anything to do with me."

"I wouldn't be too sure about that." Boone had been a handsome, caring, and gentle young man, and Jillian had a hard time believing he'd been thrown over for some wild man who seemed to have had so little substance to him. "I can't help but wonder why she never explained to her daughter who Miss Rita was after the letter came about the bequest."

"Allison didn't want to bother her mama with it. Janine has been so sick, you see. At first, Allison figured she'd come down here to Moss Hollow and get the situation with her bequest resolved, then wash her hands of the whole thing. But it's not working out that way."

"Of course not."

"But anyway, the reason I stopped by is to see if you and Savannah still want to help get Miss Rita's things packed up and disposed of. I surely could use some help. Allison is willing to let me take more time, but that Gary Moody told me I need to get everything out right away so there's no wiggle room for a lawsuit from anyone."

"Do you really think that would happen now? I mean, considering what all of us have learned?"

"He's a lawyer. It's how he views the world."

"Whatever you need, Boone, I'll be glad to help. When do you want me?"

"I'll get a little more done each day before I leave for work, but if you'd come on Saturday, I believe we can finish up."

"I'll be there."

He thrust out one hand and shook hers warmly. "Thank you, Jillian."

"You are more than welcome."

They walked back to the front of the bakery, where Bertie and Lenora made no effort to hide their curiosity.

"I'm going to help Boone finish up at Miss Rita's on Saturday," she told them after he left. "I hope you don't need me here."

"We'll manage. You go help that man," Bertie ordered.

Jillian was wrapping up the fragile collectibles in Miss Rita's living room Saturday morning when a vehicle with a tremendously loud engine roared its way into the driveway.

"What in the world?" She ran to the window. "Boone, there's a bulldozer out there!"

"I know. That shed's coming down today."

"It is?"

"It's full of rot. It's an eyesore."

"And it's probably dangerous if kids were to decide to start playing in it." Savannah brought in a large box of clothes, freshly laundered and folded.

"It's a wonder it hasn't collapsed before now," Jillian said.

Savannah blanched. "I'd hate to think of it falling in on Cherry."

Boone gave her a wry smile. "Then don't think about it. She's safe and sound in Larry Don's garage."

"As great as her place always looked, and as well as you've maintained everything for her, I'm surprised she didn't want you to build another place for that car," Savannah said.

"I know." Boone took the box of clothes and stacked it with a couple of others near the front door. "She said as long as his car was in that shed where he always parked it, she could believe he'd be coming home."

Jillian shook her head. "That's so sad."

"Before Allison left, we decided that whether she decides to keep the place or to sell it, removing the shed is an improvement."

"There's a dump truck too." Savannah pointed out the window.

Boone glanced out the window. "Yep. Gonna haul off all the debris from the shed."

Predictably, the loud machine and its destructive intent drew interest, and several neighbors stood on the sidewalk or wandered into the yard to take in the scene. The crowd included Hunter, Larry Don, Sheriff Henderson, and a couple of deputies, who must have come over from working on Cherry in Larry Don's garage.

Boone was watchful as the process began, pausing frequently to glance out the window. "I don't like the tracks that machine is making in the yard," he muttered at one point.

"It can't be helped." Jillian patted his back.

"I'll get out there with a rake as soon as they're gone and try to smooth it out," Boone said.

As the crashing, crunching noises increased, so did the worry lines in his face.

"Boone," Savannah said, "why don't you go on outside and make sure he doesn't run over the rose bed?"

He stiffened and leaned near the window, peering toward the roses.

"Go on," Jillian urged. "We'll keep packing in here."

Boone hesitated, then nodded. "Thanks, ladies. I'm sure the job won't take long."

"He is such a worrier," Savannah said after he'd gone. "I'll be glad when everything about Miss Rita's estate is settled and he can relax."

"If he takes a page from Bertie's book, he'll find something new to stew about."

"Everyone knows you're the family worrywart." Savannah tilted her head. "What in the world is everyone yelling about out there?"

"What if someone's hurt?" Jillian grabbed her phone, and they dashed outside.

The bulldozer chugged idly in place near a mound of splintered debris. Everyone now stood clustered in one place, staring at the ground, unmoving. Jillian and Savannah rushed to the group and worked their way to the front to see what had captured the attention of the others.

"What is that?" Savannah gasped, recoiling.

"It looks like . . ." Jillian swallowed hard. "It's a hand."

19

"It's the right hand." Hunter was hunkered down next to it. "Don't mess with it," he ordered sharply as Larry Don started to prod the bones with the toe of his boot.

"Step away." Sheriff Henderson's deep voice brooked no argument or hesitation. "Jones, get these gawkers out of here."

As Gooder shooed back the onlookers and instructed them to stay away, Jillian and Savannah stood close together, eyeing the goings-on. As curious and mortified as they were by the unexpected discovery, neither was inclined to get in the way of police work. Deputy Shaw took photos from every angle and caught pictures of everything Hunter pointed out.

"A dead body in Miss Rita's shed," Jillian murmured. "I wonder who it is and how long it's been there."

She and Savannah stared toward the area where Hunter and the deputies were carefully moving dirt away from more bones. Jillian shuddered.

Rod Douglas, editor and reporter for the *Moss Hollow Chronicle* walked up the driveway, camera in hand.

"Here comes the press," Jillian said. "This is newsworthy, unfortunately. Where is Boone?"

He was nowhere in sight.

"Maybe he's in the house," Savannah suggested. "Poor Boone. This is all he needs to add to his burden." She bit her lower lip. "Do you realize how many times I've said or thought 'poor Boone' in the last few weeks?"

"We all have. He's lived so quietly and so independently for so long that I think most people are hardly aware of him, and then he's thrust into all this. Let's go join him, make him feel that he has friends who care."

"I agree. In fact, I really don't want to see more bones."

In the house, the living room had finally lost its familiar, homey atmosphere, with the shelves and walls empty of Miss Rita's familiar belongings. Savannah had taken down the curtains, and without their softening effect, daylight now glared through the windows. Boxes were neatly lined up and stacked along the walls.

Boone was sitting on the sofa, staring at something in his hands.

"You okay?" Jillian asked softly, sitting next to him.

Savannah perched on his other side on the arm of the sofa.

His hands trembled, his face was white. When he lifted his head, his eyes harbored a haunted expression. He seemed to be lost inside himself.

"It's Ryan." His voice was barely audible.

Jillian glanced at the photo that had held his attention. "And you?"

"Huh?" he asked, as though speaking from someplace faraway.

Jillian dipped her head toward the picture. "Is that you with him?"

He blinked and dropped his gaze to the photo. "Yeah, me and Ryan."

"May I see it?"

He gave a barely perceptible nod and Jillian lifted it from his fingers. "Which one is you?"

"On the left. With black hair."

She smiled at the image of the two young boys. "How old were you when this was taken?"

"I dunno. Twelve maybe. Thereabouts."

"You were both cuter than bugs' ears."

He gave a slight smile. "I guess."

She handed the photo to Savannah who studied it intently. "You know what? I don't see much resemblance between Ryan and Ms. Vinton."

"Well, several years have passed, you know," Jillian said.

Savannah looked up, met her gaze, and smiled. "I know. But I thought there might be something more, in the eyes or shape of the ears."

"It's Ryan." Boone's voice had taken on the same haunted quality as his eyes.

Savannah nodded. "Yes, so you said."

"I mean it's Ryan."

Jillian and Savannah exchanged a glance, and Savannah lifted one shoulder to show her confusion.

"Right," Jillian said. "That's him on the right, you on the left."

"No, I mean *it's Ryan*."

There were a couple of raps on the front door, and Sheriff Henderson stepped inside.

"And now, you'll see what I mean," Boone said.

Something uneasy and frightening stirred to life inside Jillian. A glance at Savannah mirrored the same disquiet.

After an initial glance at the two women, Henderson more or less dismissed their presence. "We found something, Boone."

"Yes sir."

The sheriff held up a thin ball chain with two oblong metal tags hanging from it.

"Yes sir," Boone said again.

Jillian felt her eyes go big. "Those are dog tags?" she asked, her voice barely audible.

"Did you find that with the bones?" Savannah placed one hand to her lips.

Sheriff Henderson might as well have been carved from stone, and Boone from ice.

"Maybe they were just found in the debris of the shed?" Jillian sounded hopeful, but her remark hung in the air for a time.

"These were with the bones, not in the debris," the sheriff said finally. "Boone."

"It's Ryan."

Silent seconds ticked by as Jillian finally absorbed the importance of those two words.

"How long has he been there?" Henderson closed the chain and ID tags in his fist.

Boone shook his head. "Since the day he went missing, I'd guess."

The sheriff's gaze never wavered. He didn't even blink. "Uh-huh."

Silence fell again and a thread in Jillian's middle stretched tighter and tighter. "Those bones, they're Ryan Carter?"

"That's right. We found the skull. It had been smashed in."

Savannah's face paled. "Someone killed him?"

Henderson said nothing, and Jillian thought the thread might break. "Surely you don't think Boone had anything to do with that." The words burst from her mouth before she had time to consider them.

The sheriff shifted his steely gaze to her. "Best you keep out of this, Jillian."

"But, Sheriff Henderson, Boone would never—"

"Savannah."

Jillian was aghast. "We can't let you accuse—"

Henderson bristled, and Boone spoke up. "You two go on home. I have things to tell the sheriff."

Savannah scooted off the arm of the chair onto the cushion and linked her arm with his. "Nope."

Jillian edged closer to him and linked his other arm. "I'm not going either."

They both turned stubborn faces to the sheriff, who said, "You want me to haul all y'all in?"

Jillian tried to imagine how Bertie would react to that, and her resolve wavered.

Savannah apparently suffered no such qualms. "If that's what you have to do, Sheriff, but the three of us have bonded a close friendship since Miss Rita died, and we aren't going to abandon one another." She patted Boone's forearm.

Henderson narrowed his eyes at her. Rarely did anyone get away with back-talking the sheriff of Nathan County.

"You girls don't need to be getting yourselves in trouble for me," Boone said. "I'm an old man and I can take care of myself."

"You're not an old man, and we know you can take care of yourself. But we want to be here for you anyway. Miss Rita would never forgive us if we left you alone right now." Jillian surprised herself with how controlled and firm she sounded when she actually had no idea what was the right thing to do. *Yes, you stand up for your friends, but no, you don't let a guilty person go unpunished.*

Had Boone killed his friend and buried him in the shed? Was it possible?

No, it's not possible. The other day as they worked, Jillian had seen him catch a spider and release it outside. *Would a murderer do that?* "A person is presumed innocent until proven guilty," she announced.

Henderson raised one eyebrow. "Right."

"I didn't kill Ryan, if that's what you're thinking," Boone told her.

Her mouth flew open. "I never said . . . I never thought . . ." But that's exactly what was dancing around the periphery of her mind. He'd been so strange, so secretive, his actions and reactions so odd.

"Sheriff, I didn't kill Ryan, but I'm not surprised someone did," Boone said.

Sheriff Henderson dragged a chair in from the dining room, flipped it backward and straddled it. "Okay. I'm listening."

"When Ryan came home from Vietnam, Miss Rita was happier than I'd ever seen her. I figured he'd take up right where he left off, wheedling her out of everything he could, but he didn't. For a month or two, he seemed settled. Then Sonny Stonemaker showed up and Ryan was back to his old ways."

This was nothing different from the story Boone had shared at supper in Belle Haven. Jillian shifted her weight on the sofa.

"Sonny Stonemaker?" Henderson pulled out a small notebook from his pocket and made a note. "Go on."

"I hated that Sonny had come on the scene. For one thing, Miss Rita deserved to be treated with respect and kindness, and Ryan was finally acting like he had some sense. For another, Ryan and I—well, we were becoming friends like we'd been when we were kids. It was good." His eyes strayed to the photograph of them Savannah had laid on the coffee table.

"Go on." The sheriff's gaze never left Boone's face.

Boone's entire body stiffened. He clenched and unclenched his hands, and it seemed to Jillian that he had stopped breathing, as if what he was about to say might choke him. "I sorta fell in with them, I guess you could say."

The sheriff didn't bat an eyelash. "You either did or you didn't. There's no straddling the fence about that."

"I thought you said once Sonny entered the scene, that was it for you and Ryan," Jillian said.

Henderson glanced at her and Boone winced, but he did not explain or deny her words.

"I was already working at the store," Boone said. "Janine and I were talking about maybe getting married when she graduated high school, and there was Ryan and Sonny, running around without a care in the world, having a high time. You remember how Ryan was, Coy."

Henderson slightly inclined his head.

"I wasn't a good student, 'cause I can't read well, but I was always a good kid. By the time I was eighteen, I suppose I felt like I was an old man already, and I wanted to know what it felt like to let loose and be wild like that. So, yeah, that summer I kinda fell in with them."

Jillian frowned, trying to make what he was telling Henderson fit with what he'd told her, Bertie, and Cornelia.

"This 'falling in' you did, what did it consist of?" Henderson asked.

Boone squirmed between the two women and freed himself from their gentle clasps. "Some joyriding, some carousing."

"Drinking?"

"Not me."

"But the other boys did?"

"For sure."

Henderson left a silence of two beats. "Thieving?"

Boone didn't answer.

"Thieving?" Henderson said again, loudly, as if Boone might not have heard.

Boone gave the slightest nod. "Yeah. That."

"*You* stole?" Jillian fixed a shocked expression on him.

He bent his head and stared at his clenched fists. "A little."

Jillian met Savannah's eyes over Boone's head.

Henderson scratched his earlobe. "Define a little."

"We broke into the Milsaps' house while they were on vacation."

"Eddie and Trudy Milsap?"

"Eddie's folks' place. And we pilfered a few things from a couple of stores."

The sheriff said nothing. Jillian knew he was waiting, like a spider expecting prey to enter a web. But she was still having a hard time wrapping her head around the knowledge that Boone Hackett had broken the law.

"We, uh, we broke into a few houses." Boone shifted his weight and went from clenching and unclenching his hands to rubbing the knuckles of his right hand with the thumb of his left.

"Did you get into a fight?" Jillian asked, watching him.

He frowned.

"Did you?" Henderson prodded.

Boone shrugged. "I guess, yeah. A couple of times."

"Anybody hurt?"

"I don't know. Could be." He glanced up, briefly. "Those two boys were just back from Vietnam. They knew how to do it."

"What about you?" the sheriff asked.

"I stuck up for myself, but I never hurt anyone bad. A bloody nose, maybe. Nothing more. I left the hardcore stuff to the fellas who wanted to wrangle." He looked down again. "I'm not a wrangling type. Never was."

Savannah patted his arm. "Of course you aren't." She glared at the sheriff as if this were his fault.

"After a while, I didn't want to have any more to do with either of them. Ryan had sweet-talked his way into Janine's heart. About the time we broke into Stewie Franks's place was when everything changed."

Savannah's eyes widened. "You're the ones who stole from Stewie?"

"I didn't want to do it, but nothing would satisfy Sonny except to break in and find the money Mrs. Franks had hidden. And so we did. I hated it."

Jillian reared back. "How did Sonny know about that cash? Stewie didn't even know about it, and it was his wife who'd been saving it."

Boone glanced at her out of the corner of his eye. "Sonny did a little work for her at some point, hauled off some brush or something. She didn't have enough cash in her purse to pay him, so she went to get the rest, and he sneaked around and spied on her getting it out of its hiding spot in a dresser drawer. After that, wouldn't nothing do but he had to have it."

"Didn't you try to stop him?" Jillian asked, ignoring the irritated expression on Henderson's face.

"Sure. Stewie and his wife were good folks. They weren't rich, and I figured if they had money socked away, it must have taken them awhile to save it. I told Sonny that, but he didn't care. So I told him I wasn't gonna be a party to the shenanigans anymore. Told him I was gonna go to the sheriff. He laughed and said go ahead, because it was no secret what we'd been doing. Said Pointer would probably want a cut of it. He said Pointer would probably give him the key to get in and throw me in the lockup for snitching, and Ryan would be arrested for good measure. He said Miss Rita would be heartbroken if her boy went to jail." He paused. "I knew about Pointer. I believed him, and I never said anything to anyone."

Henderson cocked his head to one side, a dark scowl on his face.

Boone continued. "About a week later, Ryan came over and said he was gonna break with Sonny before things got out of hand. Sonny had been talking about doing some big stuff, dangerous stuff."

"Like what?" Henderson asked.

"Like robbing the bank in Bristow, for one. That was a sure ticket to prison, and Ryan wanted no part of it. He told me he wanted to settle down with Janine, have a proper home and raise a family."

"He had a change of heart?" Savannah asked.

Boone shrugged. "Seemed so. He'd sold what he could of the stuff we'd stolen, and he had his cut of the stash Mrs. Franks had hidden, and he said he had enough to get a start."

"That change of heart didn't extend to him giving back money and property," Henderson added.

"I wanted to believe he'd made a change, but if he was so contrite, why wasn't he trying to help his mother instead of himself? Besides, I was pretty sure he'd go back to his old ways once the shine had worn off the romance a bit. Janine was a fine girl, sweet and loving. Too good for the likes of Ryan Carter, but I reckoned he was who she wanted, and I knew she wouldn't listen to me." Boone took in and let out a deep breath. "Anyway, a couple of nights later, Sonny showed up at my house late wanting to know where Ryan kept his loot. I didn't know and told him so. He was so mad, I thought he was gonna kill me. He said if I tried to sic the law on him, Miss Rita would be the one to pay." He lifted his head, agony on his face. "The next day, Ryan was gone. He hadn't left Moss Hollow, and I knew it. I've known it all along."

20

"You believe Sonny killed Ryan?" Henderson's cold gaze bored into Boone, pinning the man in place.

Boone nodded. "I think he killed him that night, buried him in the shed, then parked the car on top of him and removed the distributor cap to disable the car in case Miss Rita or I tried to move it."

Savannah leaped to her feet and gawked at him. "Do you mean to say you have known all this time that Ryan was dead, and you've let Miss Rita live through torment, hoping and praying and watching for his return?"

"All I had were my suspicions. I couldn't prove anything."

"So what? You could have—"

Boone stood, his face red, his eyes blazing. "What was I supposed to do, Savannah? What would you have done? Gone to Pointer, who was obviously in cahoots with Sonny Stonemaker? He threatened to harm Miss Rita. Get it? He was a thug. He would have hurt her. If I'd said anything to anyone, her bones would be out there in that shed too."

Savannah stamped a foot. "But you didn't—"

Henderson stood. "That's enough. Shush, both of you. I'll be asking the questions from here on." He glowered at Savannah and Jillian. "Got it?"

Savannah sat down with a huff. "Yes sir."

He shifted his gaze to Jillian. "You?"

Chastened, Jillian shifted in her seat. "Got it."

"Boone. Sit." He pointed to an armchair. "There."

Boone grudgingly moved a packed box to the floor and sat.

"What makes you so sure he's the one who killed Ryan?" the sheriff asked.

"They both disappeared at the same time, and Ryan left his car behind. Logic would tell most people they'd left together because they were in each other's company so often, but I knew Ryan loved that Riviera and wouldn't have done that." At a raised eyebrow from the sheriff, Boone added, "I didn't know for sure Ryan was dead until you found those remains."

"And yet you said nothing, even then." Henderson studied him as if probing Boone's mind.

"I'm talking now."

"So when that lockbox was found, you knew where it came from?"

"I recognized the jewelry. I figured Ryan had hid it in the car where Sonny couldn't find it, and that's what got him killed."

The sheriff drew in such a hard breath that his nostrils pinched. "Still afraid of Sonny Stonemaker?" When Boone said nothing, he pushed further. "Seen him lately? Do you know where he is?"

"I haven't seen him since that night." The words came out even, without inflection.

"We can't find any trace of him online," Jillian said, although she risked being called out for speaking up.

"Is that right?" Henderson said mildly.

"That's right," Savannah said. "We both did extensive online searches for him. I even went through old obituary files for the state. And I asked Gooder if he could find anything in the police files."

I didn't know that, Jillian thought in surprise.

Henderson's left eyelid twitched. Jillian figured Savannah might have volunteered too much information.

"And what did Gooder tell you?"

"He said he'd check into it."

"And?"

"And he either didn't find anything or he forgot to tell me."

"So nothing?"

"Right."

Henderson wiped one hand down his face, then massaged the back of his neck. Boone vacated his seat to stand at the front window and gaze out at the hot day. Jillian cast a glance at the others in the room and wondered what each one was thinking. Surely the sheriff knew more than he was saying. But who could tell? She'd never seen his face anything but steely, and she never expected to in her lifetime.

"Are you going to arrest me, Coy?" Boone said suddenly.

"How's that?"

"For murder."

"Did you kill Ryan Carter?"

"No." Boone faced them, pain in his eyes. "But I did kill Miss Rita."

The silence was deafening, then Savannah cried, "Oh, Boone, you did not!" She turned to Henderson. "Sheriff, Jillian and I were right there next to her bed as she passed away. No one killed her."

"Why would you say such a thing, Boone?" Jillian asked.

"Because I did. As good as."

Henderson glowered at him. "What are you talking about?"

"It was me that caused it. When I saw that lockbox that had been hidden in Ryan's car, I figured it was what Sonny had wanted to find. I figured Ryan might've hidden other stolen items in the shed, and sooner or later there'd be a record of it somewhere, and I'd be found out."

Henderson made an impatient gesture. "I've been the sheriff in these parts a long time, and I've seen a lot of baloney, and you confessing to murder, Boone Hackett, is one of the biggest crocks of nothing I've ever heard."

"That's right," Jillian chimed in.

Boone sniffed. "Stewie Franks knew we took his stuff."

"*What?*" Savannah gaped at him. "How in the world would he know that?"

"Because I found out that he knew I'd pawned a watch—a stolen watch—at the local pawnshop. And he didn't say one word to me. In all these years since, he hasn't mentioned it."

"For goodness' sake." Jillian couldn't believe the flow of information coming out of quiet old Boone Hackett.

"And now I'm telling you it was me in the shed that night, trying to find anything else that might be there, because I didn't want anyone, ever, to know I used to be a thief. That's why I ransacked this place. I was afraid there might be something, somewhere."

"That night in the shed." Henderson's voice sliced through the thick, tense atmosphere of the room.

Boone swallowed hard and met his eyes. "Through the open doors, I saw the glow of someone's cell phone. I figured it was some curious kid from the neighborhood, but I didn't want to be caught, even by a kid. It was pitch-black outside. Cloudy. I knew I wouldn't be recognized in a night that dark, so I ran out. If I'd known it was Miss Rita who was coming toward the shed, if I'd realized she'd fallen . . ." His voice faltered. "It wasn't on purpose." Boone's face was ashen.

"Oh for Pete's sake," Henderson burst out in a rare show of emotion. "Sit down before you fall down. I am not arresting you for murder unless you killed Ryan Carter, which I strongly doubt you did. And no more talk of killing Miss Rita. That's hogwash, and you know it." He stood. "I'm done here. Stay with him for a bit, make sure he's okay. And try to talk him out of this notion he killed Miss Rita."

"Of course." Jillian had never realized Sheriff Henderson had so much faith in her and Savannah.

Two weeks later, the Southern Sweetie Pies meeting had just gotten underway when the bakery door opened and Boone walked in. He carried a basket with a blue-checked cloth covering the contents.

The moment he stepped across the threshold, every voice in the room hushed and all eyes fastened on him. To Jillian, he had seemed lighter in the last few weeks. He was still robust and healthy, but now his eyes sparkled and his smile reached his eyes. It had taken her and Savannah a lot of hours and plenty of tears all around to bring him to a place he finally felt at peace with himself.

"Hi." His smile was shy and endearing. "I reckon it's okay for me to show up like this? I brought something." He held up the basket.

"Why, sure you're welcome," Jillian said. "Sit here between Savannah and me." She drew up a chair for him.

"What'd you bring?" Lenora asked.

Boone stood in front of them and peeled back the bright cover. "Savannah found this recipe when we were cleaning out Miss Rita's kitchen. It was torn a little, but once Savannah read it, I remembered. These are cookie bars Miss Rita and my mama invented for me and Ryan." He paused for a flicker of a second. "They're chocolate, but among other things they have sour cream, eggs, butter, nuts, and strawberry jam."

"Mercy me," Cornelia piped up. "I gained ten pounds just listening to the list of ingredients."

Everyone laughed. Wanda Jean asked, "Did you make a copy of the recipe for us?"

"Yes ma'am. There's a whole stack of them if anyone wants one."

By the end of the meeting, Boone was more relaxed and cheerful than Jillian had ever seen him. The previous week, Sheriff Henderson had found out that Sonny Stonemaker had died in prison in 1976. The news seemed to have taken a huge load off Boone's mind, and he seemed years younger. He chatted with several of the members and was invited to return.

"So is that Vinton woman going to get rid of Miss Rita's place?" Wanda Jean asked.

"I'm not sure," Boone said. "She's still thinking about it."

"I know someone who might want to buy it, if she does."

"Oh, you do not, Wanda Jean." Maudie caught her arm. "You're just fishing for gossip. Come on, let's go. Hugh's talking about trading in our car for some jazzy little number, and I need to keep talking him out of it." She gave Boone a sour look. "Ever since you boys started working on that Riviera, all Hugh has talked about is getting himself a sporty car."

Boone laughed. "Maybe he'd be satisfied taking a ride in Cherry once in a while. I'm pretty sure Savannah would be agreeable."

"I sure would," Savannah said. "The men tell me they've got the engine running well. Just as soon as the seats are ready to be installed, you and Hugh and I will go for a nice long drive."

Maudie's face broke out into a bright smile. "We'd like that."

After everyone but Jillian, Cornelia, Bertie, and Savannah had left the bakery, Boone said, "I'm retiring."

"You are?" Cornelia blinked at him. "My goodness, the store won't be the same without you."

He smiled at her. "That's kind of you to say, Miss Cornelia, but a night manager is easily replaced."

"But still." She looked ready to shed a tear or two.

"What are you going to do?" Jillian asked.

His face turned red and he ducked his head, smiling like a

shy schoolboy. "Well, first off, I'm going to Little Rock. I'm going to go see Janine."

"You are?" A smile burst across Savannah's face. "Oh, Boone, how wonderful."

"Well, she might not be as eager to see me as I am her, but she's invited me, anyway."

"Of course she's eager to see you again," Jillian said. "Who wouldn't be?"

"Aw, well." He flushed again and shifted from one foot to the other. "I started to take all of Miss Rita's things to the charity shops, but Allison has asked me to wait. She's thinking of keeping the house as a vacation place for her and her mother. She said she'd like to use some of Miss Rita's things, as a tribute to her."

Savannah smiled. "That's a lovely idea."

"It would be great," he said. "Having Miss Rita's granddaughter there means a little bit of her will still be with us."

"So Ryan was her father, after all?" Jillian asked.

He nodded. "Yeah. Janine had meant to tell her a long time ago, but the time never seemed right, and after Thad died, she didn't have the heart. But after Allison's trip here, and her bequest, and all the unanswered questions—well, she finally confessed it all. She and Thad actually got married about a year after she left Moss Hollow, a few months after Allison was born."

"I do hope Ms. Vinton keeps the place," Savannah said. "It will be nice to get to know them."

"When I was talking with her on the phone the other day, Allison did have one request of you all."

"What's that?"

"She'd like you to call her Allison, not Ms. Vinton."

Jillian grinned. "We can do that."

"We surely can," Savannah said. "And now, Boone, I want another of those cookie bars you made. In fact, I want two."

A Dark Turnover
Book Seventeen Recipe

The Chocolate Shoppe's
Cherry Turnovers

Cherry Filling

3 cups fresh or frozen sweet
    cherries, pitted
¼ cup water
1 tablespoon lemon juice

⅓ cup granulated sugar
2 tablespoons cornstarch
¾ teaspoon vanilla

Pastry

2 frozen puff pastry sheets,
    thawed according to
    package instructions

1 egg white, lightly beaten

Vanilla Glaze

1½ cups confectioners' sugar
2 tablespoons milk

1 teaspoon vanilla

Instructions

1. To make filling, place cherries in a medium saucepan over medium heat. Add water, lemon juice, sugar, and cornstarch. Bring to a boil. Turn the heat to low and cook for about ten minutes, stirring often. Remove from heat. Stir in vanilla. Let cool.

2. Preheat oven to 375 degrees. Line two baking sheets with parchment paper. Unwrap both puff pastry sheets and cut each sheet into four squares to make eight total. Arrange squares on baking sheets.

3. Place a heaping tablespoon or two of cherry filling in the center of a pastry square. Brush the edges of the square with egg white. Fold the pastry in half diagonally, forming a triangle, to enclose the filling. Use a fork to crimp the edges shut. Repeat with all pastry squares.

4. Bake turnovers for 20 to 25 minutes, until puff pastry is golden brown. Let cool on a wire rack.

5. To make vanilla glaze, combine confectioners' sugar, milk, and vanilla in a bowl and whisk until smooth. Drizzle over the cooled turnovers.